Death in the Middle Watch

LEO BRUCE

Death in the Middle Watch

A CAROLUS DEENE MYSTERY

ACADEMY CHICAGO PUBLISHERS

FICTION

Published in 2004 by
Academy Chicago Publishers
363 West Erie Street
Chicago, Illinois 60610

Printed and bound in the USA

Library of Congress Cataloging-in-Publication Data on file
with the publisher.

ISBN 0-89733-523-6

One

"A MAN DIED ON one of our cruises a year ago," said Mr Porteous. "I don't want it to happen again."

Carolus looked at him coldly, thinking how obvious some people can be. Of course he didn't. The successful proprietor of Summertime Cruises was scarcely likely to want deaths to occur on the ships he chartered.

"How did it happen?" he asked.

"A Mr Travers. He just died. Nothing particular about it. He and his wife occupied separate cabins because he snored. The steward found him cold when he took him his tea in the morning. Might have been heart. He was a rich man too," he added as though heart disease was an affront to one who can afford to avoid it.

"What did the doctor say? Or didn't you carry a doctor?"

"Of course we did. I know the regulations. But unfortunately Dr Yaqub Ali was indisposed himself at the time. Seasick, you see. I don't know how a man can take a job as a ship's doctor when the slightest little swell turns him green and sends him to his cabin. He made an examination but I'm afraid it may have been a rather perfunctory one."

"Yet you buried him at sea?"

"His wife insisted on it. There was one thing poor Mr Travers had always wanted when he went, she said: it was to be buried at sea. He came from seafaring stock, I believe, though he himself was a bookmaker. I was against it. Rather morbid for people on a holiday cruise I thought. But the Captain persuaded me . . ."

"Oh, you were on board yourself?"

"Actually, no. But of course Captain Scorer was continually in touch with me. He considered that so far from upsetting the cruisers, as we call them, a burial at sea would make a nice change. They get rather tired of deck quoits, you know, and he would conduct the service himself as he was required to do. I considered that if that was his view he should go ahead, and afterwards we had no complaints."

"Complaints?"

"Well, cruisers are apt to complain of the slightest thing. They might have said it ruined their holiday and claimed goodness knows how much in damages. We've had that before now when a woman went mad just before we reached Las Palmas and tried to throw the baby of some other passengers overboard."

"But didn't succeed, I hope?"

"Well, no. But it was a near thing. If it hadn't been for the deck steward having the presence of mind to shout to her that her knickers were showing while the mother of the child grabbed it back I don't know what would have happened. People will complain for the slightest reason."

"But to return to the man who died. You didn't suspect what is called 'foul play', I suppose?"

"Not at the time. We thought, the doctor and all of us, that it was a heart attack. But when these letters began to arrive, I had my doubts."

"You haven't told me about those."

"You shall see them. Type cut out of newspapers. You know the sort of thing. Posted in Paddington. Threatening that the cruise would end in disaster. The sixty-fifth cruise, that is, of the *Summer Queen.* All our ships are named *Summer.* There's the *Mediterranean Summer*, the *Southern Summer*, the *Atlantic Summer.* A gimmick, of course, but it works. It was on the *Summer Queen* that the man died, and it's the *Summer Queen* sailing on June the second, that we've received these letters about. They're the reason why I've come to you."

"Have you reported them to the police?"

"Yes, but the police can't send men on a cruise, can they? It would soon get about among the cruisers. There'd be complaints at once. I thought you would never be noticed."

"I can't say I'm very keen on the idea. A cruise to Cyprus doesn't sound my idea of a holiday. Especially with . . ."

"Oh, we're not overbooked, there'll be plenty of room. You could even bring a guest."

That seemed to interest Carolus.

"If I do come," he said, "I should want to invite three guests."

"Three? I'm afraid that would entail rather a lot of expense to the company."

"Or the other hand, I should not charge a fee for my services."

"And you would try to discover what these letters are all about? You'd prevent anything more happening?"

"I can't promise that. I would do my best."

"I take it your guests would all be . . . female? They would add to the gaiety of the cruise?"

"I'm afraid not. The only female would be my housekeeper, Mrs Stick. She has been with me many years. A holiday would do her good."

"And the other two?"

"Her husband. Named Stick, naturally."

"Naturally. And the third?"

"My previous headmaster. Mr Hugh Gorringer. He might add to the gaiety of the voyage. It depends on what kind of sense of humour you have. I find him quite amusing."

"Are these the only conditions you would consider? I would prefer to pay a fee. Anything within reason."

"Mr Gorringer is certainly within reason. So are the Sticks. Yes, I'm afraid those are the only terms on which I would accompany the cruise."

"I shall have to consider it. It's our best cruise, you know. A real luxury holiday. Lisbon, Tunis, Famagusta, Gib and home. All interesting places. The longest distance we run. The net cost of three passages . . ."

"I'll leave you to decide," said Carolus. "Those will have to be my terms. And I can't promise startling results."

"You see, we don't know yet that anything very serious is going to happen. It may all be unnecessary. Your housekeeper is middle-aged?"

"Mrs Stick cannot be less than sixty."

"We need young people who dance and that sort of thing. Our officers are specially chosen."

"For what? Their looks?"

"Let's say their appeal. I have considerable experience in organizing cruises, Mr Deene. There is nothing that makes for success more than a crowd of young officers who give some attention to their passengers."

"And some, I hope, to the navigation of the ship?"

"Of course," said Mr Porteous briefly. "I suppose we shall have to agree to your terms. We must find out what these letters mean. We can't have any more heart attacks. It will give us a bad name."

"Will you accompany the cruise?"

"If you advise it, yes. I don't want to. I'm a home bird, really. Live in Sevenoaks. The wife won't come in any circumstances. She says the food upsets her."

"Why? Isn't it good?"

"Too good. Rich, you know. We pride ourselves on that. Plenty of choice. But my wife believes in simple things. Cottage pie. Fish and . . . fried potatoes. That sort of thing. You can't have that on a Cruise. There'd be complaints at once. Breakfast's the only meal when you can supply what people are used to. Otherwise an all-French menu. You should see one of them. You would hardly recognize . . ."

"I've no doubt. Mrs Stick will certainly enjoy herself."

"Mrs Stick? Oh, yes. Your housekeeper. I hope so. Perhaps she can contribute something to the ship's concert. Does she sing?"

"I don't know. I've never asked her. Mr Gorringer will be your man for that. Conjuring or ventriloquism. Most talented. But we have business to settle, haven't we? I would like to check up on the bookings. And I suppose you keep a file on the ship's personnel? I must examine these before we sail."

"Do. By all means. I shall put myself in your hands. Do you wish the crew to know that you have my authority?"

"Certainly not. I must make a firm condition that no one— absolutely no one, Mr Porteous—knows that I am anything but an ordinary passenger. I hope we are agreed on that?"

"Certainly."

"And I must tell you that I take the matter seriously."

"I'm very glad to hear it. It *is* a serious matter. You'd he surprised how quickly people imagine there's something wrong with a ship. You can't expect them to make bookings if they think they're going to be murdered, can you?"

Carolus was getting rather bored with Mr Porteous.

"I suppose not," he said.

"We must prevent anything like that happening again. These letters are most disturbing to me. Most disturbing. I'm afraid I may be blamed afterwards if anything happens for not making them public. But how can I? We should never get a booking."

To discourage Mr Porteous from continuing. Carolus asked to see the letters and spent some minutes examining them. After a silence he said, more to himself than to Mr Porteous, "You know what these remind me of? The letters Jack the Ripper frequently sent to the police."

"Jack the Ripper? Surely you are not going to suggest that these letters have been sent by a homicidal maniac?"

"I merely said that there is a resemblance between these letters and his. They are obviously intended to frighten you and anyone else who sees them. Has anyone else seen them, by the way?"

"Certainly not. They have been in my safe. You are the first person to see them." Then he added thoughtfully, "But the identity of Jack the Ripper was never discovered, was it?"

"No," said Carolus. "Not until eighty years too late. You say no one has seen these letters? But one should remember the writer himself and anyone to whom he may have shown them. You notice he says, 'I shall not be far away.'"

"Yes. What does that mean? Either he'll be on the ship or he won't."

"Exactly. But I don't like it, Mr Porteous. If the writer is a schizophrenic and has booked a passage—no, you call it a cruise, don't you?—on June the second, it may well lead to something more serious than a funeral at sea which 'makes a nice change', as you call it."

"You really think so? You don't think I should cancel the cruise? It would ruin me. It would be the end of Summertime Cruises. And after all, these letters may be nothing but the work of a madman."

"That's what I'm afraid of."

"Oh God," said Mr Porteous but with no suggestion of a call for divine help. "You make things sound worse than ever. A madman on one of our Summertime Cruises! You can't mean it, surely?"

"All I have said is that the letters you've been receiving closely resemble those sent by Jack the Ripper to the police."

"That's quite enough. Jack the Ripper! Do you know what it would mean if even a whisper of the name got out among the cruisers?"

"Nothing. They're not idiots, even if they have booked passages. But I agree that it will be best not to discuss the matter at all. I shall spend the intervening month obtaining information."

"How will you do that? You're not going to call on the cruisers, are you?"

"Certainly not. I shall employ a discreet professional. By the time we all go on board at Southampton, I shall know all that can be found out in a short time about your cruisers. And, of course, your crew."

"Anyone else?"

"Yourself. Your staff. Summertime Cruises in general."

"I hope you're joking."

"Certainly not. I never joke about murder."

"Who said anything about murder? All we have had are some threatening letters."

"*You* have. By implication. You believe that Mr Travers on that cruise last year was murdered."

"I assure you it never occurred to me. I merely thought it was unfortunate that Dr Yaqub Ali was indisposed at the time and that the man's wife was so emphatic about burial at sea."

"That's only another way of putting it. I must insist that you treat me with complete frankness, Mr Porteous, before and during the cruise."

"I should not be employing you if I didn't intend to do that."

"Thank you. I'll take charge of these letters, if you don't mind, and your passengers and crew lists. I have your private telephone number if there's anything else I need to know."

"You really anticipate trouble, don't you?"

"I'm sure *you* do, Mr Porteous. I have an open mind."

"You don't think . . . I mean one hears so much about hijacking in these days. Explosions, too. You will notice that we have an Irish family aboard. From Sandycove, near Dublin."

Carolus gave his most cryptic smile.

"Any Arab terrorists?" he asked.

"You are being facetious, Mr Deene. But there is a lady who has spent several years in Libya."

"British?"

"Of course. We should not accept bookings from the Palestine Liberation Front. We have no objection to Jews, though."

"That's kind of you."

"You know what I mean. Moshe Dayan and his kind would not be welcomed, but businessmen from Tel Aviv—that's another matter. *And* we bar all coloured people."

"Do you now? That's interesting. That may well be the key to the whole thing."

"I never know when you're serious, Mr Deene. We're very discreet about that. We make enquiries—privately, you know. You can't tell from names, nowadays. Somebody called John Heath-Wilson, for instance, may be black as your hat."

"Then you would not accept his booking?"

"No. But we wouldn't tell him so. We'd just say the cruise is over-booked."

"Very tactful of you. Has it ever occurred to you that these letters might be some sort of revenge?"

"I hardly think so. We don't advertise our principles."

"Have you ever heard of Black Power?"

"Only as a newspaper reader."

"I advise you to go into it a little more closely than that. You have, for instance, a Pakistani doctor . . ."

LEO BRUCE

9

"The only one I could obtain."

"Any other members of your crew, from Goa for instance?"

"Only in the galley. The chief cook is British. From Yorkshire. If you are supposing anything of that kind, you can forget it. My ship's personnel are loyal. Every man of them."

"Loyal to what? Or to whom?"

"The company, of course, Mr Deene. Have you never heard of commercial companies which inspire loyalty in their employees?"

"I have. They don't fill me with excitement. I shall study your crew list all the more closely now you've told me that."

"Do. Do." Mr Porteous sounded impatient. "Study it as much as you like. You won't find anything suspicious there."

"Not even Dr Yaqub Ali?"

"Certainly not. He graduated in Britain. School at Kidderminster, I believe."

"So that takes care of him?"

"Well, naturally. We can't go about suspecting everyone, can we?"

"Yes," said Carolus. "I'll see you on June the second. If not before. I'm quite looking forward to it."

"I wish *I* were. I tell you, Mr Deene, I'm scared. Thoroughly scared. And you say those letters might have been written by Jack the Ripper. What's more, you introduce the Colour Question."

"I beg your pardon. I do nothing of the sort."

"Well, racialism, then. But I've heard you're good at your job. I can't afford to ignore the danger. Let me say quite clearly that I shall consider the responsibility half yours if anything unpleasant happens."

"Oh, it will," said Carolus. "Make no mistake about that. To someone who thinks as you do, it's bound to happen. Meanwhile I'll bid you good-day, Mr Porteous."

Two

CAROLUS LEANED OVER THE rail of the *Summer Queen,* watching while the cruisers, as he had learned to call them, came aboard. The Purser stood beside him. They were near enough to the head of the gangplank to observe the features of arrivals but not so near that their conversation could be overheard.

"Yes," said Mr Ratchett, the Purser. "Mr Porteous asked me to give you any information you want. He says you're writing a book about one of our cruises. Not so very interesting, I should have thought, but perhaps you find people are always interesting, however ordinary they seem to others. Good heavens, here comes Mrs Travers!"

"You sound surprised."

"She's the widow of the man who died on one of our cruises last year. Surely Mr Porteous must have told you?"

"I believe he did mention something of the sort. So this is the lady who insisted on her husband's burial at sea?"

"She certainly did. I didn't like it. A long story about his always wishing for it. How did he know he would die at sea? Funny-looking woman, isn't she?"

Carolus saw nothing funny about the squat, severe-looking person, middle-aged and smartly dressed, indicated by Mr

Ratchett, but he nodded vaguely, and noticed that Mrs Travers came straight up to the Purser.

"Here we are again," she said giving Mr Ratchett her hand. "I'm sure you didn't expect me, did you?"

"To tell you the truth, no," said the Purser. "I was afraid you wouldn't care to come with us again, Mrs Travers."

"Mrs Darwin, now," said the lady, with a harsh little smile.

"Darwin? Mr Darwin was on the cruise last year, surely? A charming fellow."

"He was. That's how we met. After my dear Tom died, he showed me great sympathy. We've been married for six months."

"He's not with you now."

"He's been kept by important business. He's flying out to join the ship at Lisbon."

"I see. We look forward to seeing him then. May I introduce Mr Deene? He's coming with us."

"I expect we'll be seeing more of each other," said Mrs Darwin, with a rather grim smile. "Do you play Scrabble? You do? I'll take you on at that." Then to the Purser, "I'm glad you've given me an outside cabin. Captain's table, I suppose?"

"You must see the Chief Steward about that. I rather think . . ."

"I shall be very upset if there's any mistake. I said when booking that I should expect it."

Cleverly, Carolus thought, Mr Ratchett turned to greet another couple who had approached him.

"Sir Charles! Lady Spittals! Glad to see you again. You were with us last year, weren't you?"

Sir Charles was a disappointed-looking man, but his wife was an enthusiast.

"Well, well!" she cried. "What a nice surprise! You're looking ever so well, too. Remember the Gala Night? I think

Charles"—she dug her husband in the ribs—"was the only one who didn't enjoy himself! But then he never does. Do you? He's just the same old misery. I don't know why he comes on a Cruise like this, I really don't. He never participates in anything. All he does is sit there moping. Where have we been placed in the dining room? Are we really? Captain's table! I'm ever so glad. Not that I should have blamed you if you'd put us somewhere else with *him* sitting there looking like a funeral. Well, cheerio for now. Be seeing you."

"Strange couple," commented Mr Ratchett to Carolus. "Lord Mayor of some town up North. Knighted for his work for charities. Stinking with money. Did you notice her diamonds? They're real, I'm told. Who on earth is this?"

Mr Ratchett might well ask, for mounting the gangplank as though he was being televised, came a tall man wearing a brand-new yachting cap. Even before he saw the features, Carolus was certain that it was none other than the headmaster of the Queen's School, Newminster. It was he who introduced the Purser.

"Mr Hugh Gorringer. Mr Ratchett," he said. "Mr Gorringer is a well-known educationist."

"You flatter me, my dear Deene. If a little of the distinction of the school I serve has rubbed off on its headmaster, it is all I ask."

The Purser nodded politely. He looked as though he believed he had met this kind before, which Carolus thought scarcely possible.

"An enchanting prospect you lay before us," Mr. Gorringer continued to the Purser. "A veritable magic carpet, eh Deene? Lisbon! Tunis! Cat . . ."

"Mr Ratchett knows the route," put in Carolus.

"Of course. I'm sure he does. The voyage, not the 'route,' Deene. We must remember we're at sea now, or soon will be.

As a writer, albeit of popular fiction, you cannot afford to make errors in maritime terminology." He pulled Carolus aside. "By the way, my dear Deene. A small point but not a negligible one. I feel it due to the honour not of myself but of the school that I should be seated in the dining hall. . . ."

"We're together," said Carolus incisively. "At the Chief Engineer's table."

"I was going to say when you interposed with that information that I felt it my due, in the position I occupy, to be invited . . ."

"Next to me, Chief's table." Carolus said rather brutally.

". . . to occupy no less a place than that on the left-hand side of the Captain. Doubtless some distinguished lady will sit on his right."

"Can't be done, I'm afraid. Competition too keen."

Mr Gorringer looked hurt.

"I accept your explanation," he said. "But I should have thought . . . However."

"See you at dinner," promised Carolus cheerfully. "You'll be all right."

"I make no secret of my disappointment," said Mr Gorringer, "but I suppose I am scarcely in a position to complain since the Company, er . . . Summertime Cruises, Isn't it? . . . has been good enough to invite me as a tribute to Scholarship. Most appropriate. Very well then, we will meet at dinner, unless perhaps we might indulge in a cocktail as it is the first night on board?"

"Right. The bar then. Seven-thirty," said Carolus, turning again to Mr Ratchett who had been approached by a tall thin girl with spectacles and loose but somewhat feeble strands of mouse-coloured hair.

"Miss Berry is going on one of our Cruises for the first time," explained Mr Ratchett when he had introduced them.

"I've been with the Tropical people and with Round-the-World-Away Cruises," said Miss Berry toothily. "So I thought I'd try this. They say they get a very lively crowd."

"I feel sure they do," said Carolus. "Mr Porteous tells me he aims for that."

"Good-O!" said Miss Berry. "I'm all for some fun, aren't you? But I hope it's not too rough."

"The fun or the sea?" asked Carolus.

Miss Berry laughed.

"I can see you know your way about," she said. "The fun, of course. There were some skinheads on the *Adelphi* last year. That's a Tropical Cruises ship, but they don't go further south than Casablanca. These skinheads, quite educated they were, tried to get hold of me one night. One of them said something about a gang bang, whatever that may be."

"I hope you managed to escape?"

"Yes I did. But only because a girl who worked in the sick bay came by and they went after her. She was blonde and wore a lot of makeup. She didn't seem to mind and of course I was delighted."

"Of course," said Carolus.

"Where are you sitting in the dining saloon? I expect I'm at the Captain's table—being alone on board."

"I expect you are," said Carolus, comfortingly but insincerely. "I shall see you there."

"Ta ta for now," said Miss Berry.

"I know her sort," said the Purser sourly when she had gone. "There's a rude name for her. A something teaser. Hullo, I wonder who these are?"

Another couple, three single men, two girls and yet another couple came by and departed to search for their cabins. Then Mr Ratchett said, "This is the Dunleary family that Porteous has got such a wind up about. He's had all their luggage searched for bombs. Windy bastard. They're just a noisy middle-class Irish family. No harm in them at all. But what about these? Pretty sinister, if you ask me."

"These" were the Sticks, dressed for foreign travel. Mrs Stick, for some reason unknown as yet to Carolus, had exchanged her steel-rimmed glasses for ones with dark lenses, and Stick looked about him suspiciously. They gave no sign of recognition to Carolus, but as they passed him Mrs Stick whispered—or would it be more correct to say "hissed"?—"See you later, sir. Mustn't stop now."

"I should think," said the Purser jovially to Carolus, "I should think you'd get some pretty good copy out of this lot, one way or another. I wonder where they dig them up from?"

"Your cruises are advertised quite widely," said Carolus, then added, "I thought you didn't take coloured people?"

A very dark African-looking man was approaching.

"Oh, you mustn't take any notice of Porteous. The girls in the office have put a stop to that sort of thing this summer. They threatened to report him to the Race Relations Board and he had to give in."

"I congratulate the girls in the office."

"Old hat, that sort of thing. All the kitchen staff are Goanese and first-rate they are, so what the hell? This one who's just coming aboard is a West Indian. Alexander Carlisle, his name is. I've put him at the Captain's table next to Porteous. That'll teach old P a lesson."

"Mr Porteous explained to me how loyal everyone was to the Company, by which I took it he meant himself."

"Are they, hell? But we all have our illusions. I don't know who this man is coming up now." Mr Ratchett consulted a list. "I think his name is Stopford. I can't know everyone by name. Good evening. Mr Stopford," he called cheerily.

The man who had approached gave him a very hostile look from two steel-grey eyes.

"Runwell," he corrected.

"Of course, Mr Runwell."

"Doctor," the man reproved him again.

"Yes. I remember now. I hope you'll have a pleasant trip, Dr Runwell."

"I'm taking it purely for my health," said the other severely, as he passed on.

"What can you say?" the Purser asked Carolus with a chuckle. "Now this one just approaching is crackers. Barking. Up the wall. We had him a year ago. Wait till you hear him."

The cruiser, a powerful-looking fellow in his forties, informed the Purser that the ship ought to be taken out of commission.

"The breaker's yard is all it's fit for."

"You'll pardon the question, Mr Medlow, but why do you book a passage on her in that case?"

Mr Medlow stared.

"Why do I book a passage? Why? You know very well. I have to make my report. You're perfectly aware of that. And 1 shan't be deterred from it, either. The truth, the whole truth . . . By the way, is Mrs Grahame-Willows coming on this cruise?"

"I don't know," the Purser said. "I'll look her up." He again consulted his papers. "Yes. I think so. Her name's down, anyway."

"Strange," said Mr Medlow. "I thought she never gave her own name in any circumstances."

"Here it is—Mrs Agatha Grahame-Willows. That's her. Couldn't very well be any confusion over a name like that. could there

"You never know," Mr Medlow told him. "I shall recognize her in any case. If there's anything like impersonation I shall inform you. Is this man a private detective?" He looked at Carolus.

"Mr Deene is a passenger."

"You're not taking any precautions, then?"

"We always do that, Mr Medlow."

As he passed on, Carolus realized that the stream of cruisers had dried up. The gangplank was empty and no one was crossing from the Customs sheds.

"That's about the lot of them, I suppose," said the Purser. "May be a few last-minute arrivals, but you've seen the best of them now. All I can say is I wish you luck with that bunch. Novelist, are you? You need to be a science fiction writer, I should think."

As Carolus turned away, two of the last-minute arrivals hurried up—a man and a woman who showed no sign of being together except by the coincidence of coming at the same time. The man was young, rather good-looking in a Latin sort of way, the woman looked slightly older but still in her twenties and plump. They parted at the top of the gangplank.

"No need of his type," said the Purser, who had returned to Carolus's side. "Plenty of them among the officers. As for her, there's always one of them."

"One of them?"

"The life and soul of the party. You'll see. Not bad, was she?"

"I thought that role was reserved for Miss Berry?"

"She'd like it to be," said the Purser before he disappeared into his cabin at the top of the companionway leading down to the dining saloon.

At five o'clock in the afternoon the ship sailed, and at some time in the small hours of the morning, Carolus awakened with a start, though he had no idea what had disturbed him. He switched on the light and examining his watch found it was ten to four.

"Must be well out at sea," he thought, though he had little or no technical knowledge of seamanship.

But something had roused him. He knew himself well enough to be aware that he did not wake at this sort of time unless a sound or movement broke through his consciousness. When he heard a cry, seeming far away and rather desperate, he knew at once that it was a repetition of the sound that had aroused him. He sat up and strained to hear it yet again, and did so.

"Man Overboard!" someone was shouting and once more, it seemed with pathos and despair, "Man Overboard!"

There were sounds of running footsteps on the deck above him and a few shouted orders. He thought he heard Mr Porteous's voice, but that might have been his imagination. Then he began to dress.

Three

WHEN CAROLUS CAME OUT on deck, he noticed that the lights had been switched on, though it was still dark in the saloon. He was able to see three men in a group at the for'ard end of the deck but, hesitating behind a stack of deckchairs lashed together, he was not seen by them.

One was Mr Porteous in a dressing gown of Chinese design. The second, in uniform, was recognizable by his gold braid as the Captain, whose name Carolus knew was Scorer. The third was a sailor, what he believed would be termed a deckhand. They were holding a serious but seemingly unhurried conference. Carolus was unable to catch their words but it seemed that the Captain was giving some impressive instructions to the deckhand. No one was scanning the sea, as Carolus had expected. No one seemed concerned with anything connected with the cries that had awoken Carolus.

He waited a few moments more, hoping that the three would move within earshot. Then he walked forward boldly towards the group.

Mr Porteous turned to him.

"Hullo, Mr Deene. You're up early," he said.

"Early? You don't think I get out of my bed at this hour for amusement, do you?"

"It did strike me as strange. Let me introduce Captain Scorer, by the way. This is Mr Carolus Deene."

Carolus scarcely acknowledged the introduction.

"I was awoken by someone shouting 'Man Overboard!'" he said, with a note of accusation in his voice. He seemed to anticipate denials.

"Man Overboard?" repeated Porteous incredulously.

"You must have been dreaming," said the Captain.

"I know the difference between dreaming and reality. I distinctly heard someone shout the words. One doesn't dream that sort of thing—or I don't. If I dream I don't dream in clichés. 'Man Overboard' is a feature of every old-fashioned novel, shouted in exactly that tone of voice. What happened?"

Both Porteous and the Captain smiled.

"Nothing whatever, Mr Deene."

"Then why the conference?"

"I don't think you need concern yourself with that. Captain Scorer was giving some instructions to this deckhand, who was just going off watch. You wouldn't know that, would you? The Middle Watch changes at four o'clock and the Morning Watch comes on."

"That has nothing to do with what I heard. Have you, or have you not, been given the alarm that someone is overboard?"

"We have not," said the Captain.

"So whoever shouted did so in a nightmare?"

"I don't know about that. I can only tell you that I've been on the bridge since midnight and heard nothing of the sort."

"Yet I, in a cabin with the porthole closed, could hear it distinctly."

"Did you hear anything else?" asked Porteous. Carolus thought that there was anxiety in his voice.

"Among other things, your voice shouting."

"My voice! But I wasn't here at the time!"

Carolus turned on him sharply.

"At what time?" he snapped.

"The time you're talking about. When you imagined you heard shouts."

Carolus looked coldly at Mr Porteous.

"I should like to speak to you alone," he said.

At once the Captain, as though relieved, left them and the deckhand followed.

"I think it was agreed," said Carolus, "that you should treat me with complete frankness if I came on this cruise."

"Of course . . ."

"Then why are you concealing something as important as these events?"

"I assure you . . ."

"But you don't. There was an alarm of 'Man Overboard' tonight, and you know it . . ."

Mr Porteous seemed cornered. He proposed a drink in his cabin—where, be said, they could discuss the whole matter. Carolus acquiesced, but remained inflexible.

"Let us hear the truth," he said.

"We have no proof," Mr Porteous told him.

"Of what?"

"That . . . anything untoward took place. The deckhand, an excellent fellow called Leacock, only assumed that it had happened."

"Go on."

"He was making his rounds before going on watch. In the saloon he found this cruiser in darkness, fast asleep.

"I wish you would call him a passenger."

"Passenger, then. Fast asleep."

"Who was it?"

"That's what we don't know. Leacock described him as being tall and thin, but as Leacock is on the short side, he might think anyone was tall. It means nothing."

"You didn't see the man?"

"No. It had happened before I came on deck."

"*What* had happened, for God's sake?"

"Leacock shook the man's shoulder and told him it was just on four in the morning. The . . . passenger seemed surprised and stood up as though to go to his cabin. He said 'Thank you' to Leacock and seemed to be all right, so Leacock left him and continued his rounds. He was on the port side of the ship (he had opened the saloon door on the starboard side) when he distinctly beard a stifled cry and a splash. It is, as you will have noticed, an uncommonly quiet, still night. I should have been delighted, if it hadn't been for all this. A calm sea on the first night out of a cruise is a blessing. But tonight I can't feel that at all. Leacock hurried to the spot where he had been talking to the passenger and found him gone."

"Naturally. To his cabin."

"No. He had been wearing a raincoat and it was hanging over the rail with a jacket under it and a pair of shoes was there too. At that point Leacock gave the shout you heard. He thought the passenger had thrown himself overboard. He followed instructions and immediately threw one of the life belts into the sea so the passenger might be able to reach it. In cases like this a strong swimmer has been known to do that, though the chances are very much against it. At this point I came on deck and found Captain Scorer already there."

"He stopped the engines of course?"

"Well, no. We know from experience . . ."

"What experience?"

"Sea-going experience, Mr Deene."

"I didn't know you had any."

"The Captain certainly has. He told me that the chances were one in a hundred thousand of being able to pick anyone up, even if someone had gone overboard. Remember, we had no proof of that. He consulted me and I decided that, with the responsibility of the happiness of all the cruisers on my shoulders (they need their holidays, remember), I would avoid the panic and distress that an incident like this might cause them. The man, whoever he was, evidently wanted to die; who was I to interfere with his determination?"

"So you told the Captain to signal Full Steam Ahead?"

"Exactly. It was the only thing to do."

"Without even knowing who, if anyone, had gone overboard?"

"There were the clothes."

"I can think of a dozen explanations for those. And anyway, how do you know that he threw himself over? Leacock spoke of a stifled cry. How do you know the man was not murdered?"

"Murdered? You know, I think you are obsessed with murder, Mr Deene. The cruiser was alone, sleeping in the saloon . . ."

"But how do you know he was alone? There are so many possibilities. He might have been drugged. Another passenger might have been concealed in the saloon. He could have been thrown over the side. For all you know Leacock himself might have killed the man."

"Preposterous. Leacock's an excellent fellow."

"And thoroughly loyal, of course."

"Of course. You evidently like letting your imagination run away with you."

"But let us return to probabilities. It seems likely that one of the passengers, either deliberately or not, let himself be locked in the saloon when the lights were turned out."

"That may well be so."

"And that Leacock found him there and woke him?"

"That's what Leacock says and I'm inclined to believe him."

"Then Leacock left him and the passenger presumably took off his overcoat, jacket and shoes and went overboard to a watery grave. In that case there remain some questions for you, Porteous. Who was this passenger? Why did he want to commit suicide? Why come on a holiday cruise to do it?"

"No doubt these questions will be answered in the morning when we see which of the passengers is missing."

"But how do you know you'll see? It may not have been a passenger. A good many people were on board yesterday who weren't going on the cruise. One of them could easily have stayed on in hiding."

"You have the most extraordinary knack of making things more complicated than they are. I feel sure the mystery, such is it is, will be cleared up in the morning. The Purser has a complete passenger list and it can easily be checked. Besides . . ." there was triumph in Mr Porteous's voice, "we have all their passports."

"I agree that not much can be done tonight. I gather your conscience is quite easy about leaving the man, if there was a man, to drown?"

"It's something everyone who charters a ship may have to face at one time or another. This kind of thing is not so infrequent as you suppose. Of course I'm sorry for the poor fellow. He must have suffered a great deal before he was driven to it. But to answer your question, yes, my conscience is quite clear."

"You don't feel you should have lowered a boat?"

"Good heavens, no. You landsmen talk of lowering boats as though it were an easy matter. The whole ship would have become aware of it."

"Why not?"

"Because I had the happiness of two hundred people to think of. I had to think of them. I wasn't going to have their rest and contentment jeopardized because some lunatic decided to do himself in. And now I think we should say good-night."

"I agree. I hope you sleep well," said Carolus bitterly.

Back in his own cabin, lying sleepless in his bunk, Carolus felt for the first time since he had agreed to accompany the cruise that it might be a far more harrowing experience than he had supposed. There was now that element of the sinister which always intrigued him in cases he had to investigate. The unlighted saloon, the sleeping passenger, the stifled cry . . . and all the questions that arose from these. This was going to be no ordinary puzzle, and his instincts, sure guides to Carolus in almost every circumstance, told him that there was a—well, call it a scent of danger in the air. The three men he had found on deck had at first undoubtedly meant to keep all suspicion from him. The Captain, particularly, had been able to assume an air of innocence and denial. From Porteous he expected that, from what he had seen of the man already, but Captain Scorer, bluff, purple-cheeked, apparently plainspoken, seemed the last man to wish to hush up something that might be dangerous to his ship. As for Leacock—he was either the simple honest sailor that he appeared or else something very different. Very different indeed.

When Carolus at last dropped off to sleep, it was not for long. At half past eight he felt hungry and in need of fresh air, and going on deck found, as he expected to find at this hour and in that place, the headmaster of the Queen's School Newminster taking his morning exercise.

"Ah, Deene! A good morning to you! I fear you must keep up with my pace if we are to converse. I have still eight rounds of the deck to complete for the mile I have set myself before breakfast. I trust it will not incommode you?"

Carolus fell in beside Mr Gorringer obligingly.

"I voice no suspicion of a derogatory nature," said the headmaster as they walked. "But when I learned the welcome fact that you were accompanying this cruise I could not help but suppose that you had been drawn to it by something in

the nature of a . . . mystery, shall I say? You see, I know you of
old, my dear Deene, and I said at once to Mrs Gorringer, surely
the good Deene would not accompany a holiday cruise with
no more inducement than fresh air?"

"What did your wife say?"

"I have to confess that for once she was at a loss. But after
some discussion we decided that you must have a reason for
taking a holiday of which the means is contrary to all precedent."

"Perhaps," said Carolus. "Did you hear anything in the
night?"

"Hear anything? The ship's engines, of course. What should
I have heard?"

"Oh, nothing of any consequence."

"You cannot deceive me, my dear Deene. Your whole manner tells me that something, as they say, is going on aboard
this ship. Am I not to share your confidence? You know well
by now that no one is more worthy of it."

"You're bound to know sooner or later. You would have
heard already, probably, if you had talked to other passengers
this morning. It appears that a man may have been lost overboard last night."

Mr Gorringer paused, even halted his walk for a moment.

"Lost?" he repeated. "Overboard? A man? This is indeed
grave news. Was the poor fellow rescued?"

"No. They don't even know his identity."

"You alarm me, Deene. Do you mean to tell me that any
one of the passengers can disappear into the sea without it
being known who or for what reason? That they cannot be
found by a quickly launched lifeboat? In a word, that we are
all in danger?"

"Certainly not. If a man was lost last night . . ."

"A moment, Deene. You say a man. You appear to be certain that it was a man. Is there any reason why it should not have been a woman?"

It was Carolus who paused now and eyed Mr Gorringer fixedly.

"Good heavens!" he said.

"I see I have disturbed your complacency, Deene. Only too often we assume the masculine gender. Have I hit the nail on the head?"

"No, I'm afraid not. That wasn't what made me pause. But we *do,* as you say, assume the masculine gender far too often. Really, you know, sir, you're an extraordinary man. Quite extraordinary. You said a woman, didn't you? Just like that. Thank you!"

"I should feel more gratified by your thanks if you had not at once denied the probability of what I had voiced," said Mr Gorringer, a trifle sulkily.

"Well, yes. What you had actually said, yes. But you do throw out some interesting thoughts. And now if you have completed your walk, shall we go down to breakfast?"

"By all means. I'm delighted to have aided you, even if it was not quite as I supposed. And I'm pleased that you have so far confided in me as to admit that there is more in this cruise than meets the eye. At least that was your inference."

"Yes. But let's say no more about it."

They entered the dining room together.

Four

After breakfast Carolus was approached by Mrs Stick. Her glasses were so dark that Carolus wondered how she could have seen through them sufficiently to recognize him.

"We better go through to the Sun Lounge, sir," she said secretively. "There's so many children in there we shan't be recognized."

Carolus understood neither the logic of what she said nor the necessity for so much discretion, but he followed his housekeeper obligingly.

"You see?" she said when they had found two wicker chairs among a mass of parents and children with voices of all calibres. "We'll be able to talk without anyone overhearing here."

"Yes, but what's all this about? Why the secrecy, Mrs Stick?"

"I wasn't going to be the one to give you away," she explained. "I said to Stick, there's something funny about all this, I said. Asking us to go cruising half round the world. He must be on to something, I said to Stick."

"And what did he say?"

"He's not a man for saying much, as well you know, sir, but he agreed with me."

"He usually does, doesn't he?"

"It's not to say he hasn't got a will of his own," said Mrs
Stick defensively. "He can be very awkward at times, can Stick.
But this time there weren't two ways about it. As if we didn't
know by now when you was getting yourself mixed up in things
you ought to leave to the police. So when we heard you'd
asked us to have a holiday cruise I knew what was going to
happen."

"And what is?"

"Murder, very likely. And goodness knows what else. It
gives me the cold shivers to think of it. What about this poor
fellow last night? I said to Stick, it's soon started, I said. We'd
scarcely got out of Southampton before there was one gone."

Carolus knew that nowhere does the grapevine flourish
more than on board ship during a holiday cruise, but this
frankly surprised him.

"What poor fellow?" he asked.

"As if you didn't know. Throwing himself into the sea at
four o'clock in the morning when there was no one to rescue
him and the ship not even stopping to pick him up. Disgraceful,
I call it, and I don't care who knows it. But I suppose you'll say
he didn't throw himself in, but someone else came up behind
him when he wasn't looking? You must have your murder,
mustn't you? You'd never be satisfied with what everyone else
thinks is a suicide, and no one to blame but himself."

"Who is 'everyone,' Mrs Stick? How did you know about
it at all?"

"There's a lady at the table where we sit who heard all about
it and told us before Stick had finished ordering his sausages.
What's more, she thinks she may have seen the man who Went.
She saw someone acting very funny earlier on, dodging round a
corner, out of the way. She didn't recognize him but it may have
been the man. It was all over the ship by the time breakfast was
finished. The only thing they don't know is who it was."

"Which one? The one who dodged round the corner or the one who Went?"

"It may well have been the same, according to the lady at the table where we sit," said Mrs Stick becoming more than ever confidential in her manner. "But then I did hear it wasn't a man at all but some poor lady who'd been pushed over. It gives me the creeps to think about it. They say she'd just got up for a breath of fresh air . . ."

"At four o'clock in the morning?"

"Well, that's what they say, when this fellow crept up behind her and before you could say knife she was over the rail and into the water and drowned. But this lady at the table where we sit says it wasn't like that at all. She says it was the ship's doctor who's an Indian gentleman . . ."

"Pakistani."

"Well, it's all the same . . ."

"Oh no, Mrs Stick. Believe me, it's not. It might have been once, but it's very different now."

"Anyway, this lady at the table where we sit says he'd given drugs to some poor man. It won't be the first time, she says. She says she was on the ship last year when a man was murdered and pushed over the side before he'd been properly examined to show how it was done, she says. I suppose this doctor does it every cruise. The lady at the table where we sit thinks so, anyway."

"She seems to be rather an alarmist."

"Well, hasn't she got a right to be? I told you what she'd seen earlier, this man acting funny and dodging round corners out of sight. She thinks that doctor murders someone every time the ship goes on a cruise. She had an idea she'd seen that man before somewhere."

"Which man? The one who was acting funny or the one who Went?"

"The one who dodged round the corner."

"She doesn't think the one who Went was murdered by the doctor, does she?"

"Well, you couldn't be surprised if she was to think so, could you? If I was to tell her about you being on board, with all the experience you've had of murders and that, I don't know what she'd say."

"I hope you do nothing of the sort."

"Of course I shan't. I've told you we mustn't be seen talking or everyone will know and we don't want that, do we? Nice thing it would be if people was to hear you'd been mixed up in goodness knows how many cases before this one."

"Which one?" Carolus demanded with a provocative smile.

"This one that's going on now. Thank goodness the cabin door will lock, that's all. I couldn't sleep a wink if it wouldn't, same as I used to be at Newminster when I never knew who was coming to the door next."

———

Nothing noteworthy seemed to happen during that day. The ship continued on a southerly course in strong sunshine, and Carolus managed to avoid competitive games of all kinds though he had to make for cover once or twice on the appearance of young men with lists, seeking their prey. He slept well that night, but after breakfast, when Mrs Stick came to report to him in the Sun Lounge, he could tell as soon as she approached that she had news for him.

It appeared that the passenger, invariably referred to as "the lady at the table where we sit," had been very funny that morning.

"You could tell there was something wrong as soon as she came down. She never said a word all the time she was having her grapefruit juice that she always starts with, and when I asked her if she wasn't feeling well, she said, quite well, thank you, as much as to say 'you mind your own business.' Of course I knew I should have to get it out of her and sure enough when we were left at the table alone together, Stick not liking to light his pipe till he's out on deck, it all came out."

Carolus remained silent.

"It gave me the shudders when she told me, but I don't suppose it will to you, you being used to murders and that. It seems it was not long gone midnight when she saw the handle of the cabin door slowly moving."

"Her light was on, then?"

"Oh, yes. She keeps that on all night just In Case. She was reading a book when it happened and she says she was like someone being hypnotized. She didn't seem able to move or open her mouth or reach for the bell or anything. She just lay there watching to see what would happen next."

This time Carolus could not resist a small prod.

"And what did?" he asked.

"It was this fellow."

"Which fellow?"

"He had a white jacket on like one of the stewards, but he wasn't one at all."

"How did she know?"

"As soon as she looked, there was his grey flannel trousers. You can't tell me any of the stewards would be allowed to walk about like that. Besides, she'd never seen him before."

"What did he look like?"

"Horrible, she says. A kind of sneaky look about him as though he wanted to stick a knife in her. And still she couldn't scream. She tried to, but it wouldn't come. So all she could do was to lie there looking at him, and him looking at her, and if looks could kill—"

"Yes. I see the situation. What happened?" asked Carolus.

"All of a sudden he seemed to collect himself as you might say, turned round and went off as if someone was after him."

"So now the lady at the table where you sit was able to ring for the real steward?"

"No, she didn't. It was a choice of that or locking the door, and that's what she decided and in my opinion it was the best thing she could do. How was she to know that if she rung her bell this other one wouldn't come back to answer it? Then where would she be? So she jumped out, locked the door and jumped into bed again. Of course that's what she ought to have done in the first place."

"Undoubtedly," said Carolus.

"But I haven't told you the funny part. This wasn't meant to be her cabin, not before she came on board the ship. She'd been given another cabin which she didn't fancy because the washbasin had to be repaired. It wouldn't have taken a minute, as I told her, and they keep men specially for anything like that. Then she wouldn't have had all this trouble. But she went to the Chief Steward, he calls himself, and he said she could have the double cabin meant for a Mr and Mrs Darwin, him having cancelled at the last minute, and her having been put in a single cabin somewhere else. Another funny thing is this Mrs Darwin is the very woman whose husband died and was buried at sea list year that I told you about.

"It's my idea," went on Mrs Stick, "that whoever he was that came creeping in expected to see this man Darwin and as likely as not murdered him."

"Really, Mrs Stick, once you get the idea of murder you seem to see it everywhere. You hear of a steward wearing grey flannel trousers and you think it means . . ."

"Well, you must own it's funny. They all wear black. And the lady at the table where we sit said he looked horrible, like one of those you read about attacking anyone in railway carriages. You can think what you like, sir, but even Stick, who doesn't listen to a lot of nonsense, thinks there's something funny going on."

"I suppose the lady at the table where you sit didn't recognize the man who came to her cabin?"

"No. She didn't."

"It was not, for instance, the man who she saw 'behaving in a funny way' when she had gone on deck the previous evening?"

"Not unless he'd grown a beard in the meantime. This one she said who looked horrible had a beard, like a lot of the stewards."

Carolus thanked her for informing him so promptly and went in search of Mr Porteous. He found him being expansive at the bar.

"Have one?" he asked Carolus. "I know it's a bit early . . ."

"Porteous, I've come to the conclusion that our attempts to hush things up are useless. Everyone on board knows about the incident, whatever it was, of the night before last and it will be only a question of time before they realize that I'm here to watch things for you. I think we should anticipate that and tell them what my job is. They may have useful information."

"Aren't you rather rushing things? We know now that no one is missing."

"You do?"

"Yes. Passenger list complete."

"Then how do you account for the clothes left by the ship's rail, the stifled cry and the rest?"

"I'm afraid Leacock must have imagined the stifled cry. Unless, of course, someone was attempting to stow away and when he found he was discovered made an end of himself."

"It sounds most improbable. You think it was a stowaway who . . ."

"It seems the only solution."

Carolus looked rather serious.

"In that case I should like to examine the overcoat, jacket and shoes."

"I'll have them taken to your cabin at once, but I may tell you there's nothing noticeable about them. Not even a name-tab and nothing in the pockets."

"That in itself is noticeable. But what I want you to do is this. Tell the Captain, and anyone else you think should know, exactly what I'm doing here, and ask them to give me any assistance they can."

"Yes. I agree to that," said Mr Porteous as though he was making a large concession.

"And I want to have a talk with that deckhand, Leacock."

"I don't know what you'll gain by it but I see no objection."

"This morning?" stipulated Carolus.

"I daresay that can be arranged."

Carolus nodded and after some time went to his cabin where he found, thrown carelessly across the bunk, a brown raincoat and a tweed jacket. A pair of black shoes were beside the bunk on the floor.

He set to work to make a close examination of these and found, as he rather anticipated, that a maker's name had been removed from behind the collars of both the jacket and rain-coat, denoting, he decided, that the jacket was a product of mass tailoring. He felt inside the wallet pocket but no tailor's name had been removed from there.

Otherwise, nothing. Every pocket was empty and only a forensic examination by experts was likely to reveal anything more. The shoes gave him no more information than the clothes, though here, he knew, he was more at a loss. An ex-amination not necessarily in the police laboratories would re-

veal a great deal about the man who had worn them, probably his habits, certainly his walk. But Carolus was no microscope or magnifying-glass man. He trusted little more than
his instincts, his gift of logic and insight into motives. These
pieces of possible evidence meant nothing to him. He decided
that before he was likely to make any further progress, he
must wait for the man Leacock. Of him he had great hopes.

Meanwhile he went out on deck and was in time to hear
an announcement made over the loudspeaker system which
was audible in every part of the ship. He had been dismayed,
when he had first come on board, to hear the self-consciously
refined voice of a female member of the staff giving instructions with exaggerated politeness.

"Will all cruisers please take their passports to the office
in the central lobby?" she had said ingratiatingly. "Will Mr
Rutherford kindly come to the Purser's office immediately,
please?" And so on.

Now it was a male voice, loud and commanding as befit-
ted the Captain of the *Summer Queen*.

"This is your Captain speaking," he announced. "I want
first to wish you all a very happy cruise and to assure you that
we on our side will do everything we can to make it a pleasant
one.

"It appears that certain rumours have been circulating and
those of you who have been on cruises before will know that
this is unfortunately no rarity. Somehow things get about which
have no foundation in fact, and we who are responsible for
giving you a good time do what we can to prevent them. Let
me say at once that the story of someone calling 'Man Overboard' in the small hours of yesterday morning was a very
foolish practical joke on the part of one of the cruisers. Nothing of the sort had any basis in fact, and such tricks will not be
repeated. Summertime Cruises take every precaution to pre-

vent that sort of thing, so I hope that if any of you have felt the least alarm, you will now relax and enjoy yourselves. Thank you for listening and have a good time."

There was, Carolus noticed, silence among the cruisers who had heard this announcement, and he wondered whether it was a reflection of scepticism. He would have liked to have heard what the lady at the table where we sit had to say about it.

Five

Leacock gave a double bang on the cabin door.

"Captain says you want to speak to me," he said.

He was a powerful man, but not heavy. His hands were enormous and his neck was like rope.

"Something about the night before last, wasn't it?" he continued, as Carolus silently observed him.

"No," said Carolus finally. "About last night." Watching Leacock, he saw that he was more than surprised; almost, he thought, startled. But he might be gaining the wrong impression. "Were you on the Middle Watch again?"

"No, sir. On the First Night Watch. Off at twelve o'clock."

"I see. Were there many passengers about when you went round the saloon?"

"It was empty. No one asleep there *this* time. I didn't see a soul about."

"None of the stewards?"

"No. If the passengers have all gone to bed they go off duty about eleven."

"There wasn't, for instance, a man half dressed in steward's uniform?"

Leacock grinned.

"Now I see what you're getting at. I heard about that lady saying someone had come to her cabin half in uniform."

41

"How did you hear that?"

"Now, sir." Leacock spoke as though to a child. "You should never ask anyone how he heard things on a ship like this. Everything goes round. Passengers, crew, no one can help hearing things. One of the stewards told me as a matter of fact about this old biddy imagining a man coming into her cabin. Wishful thinking, he said it was."

"She said he had a beard."

"Very likely. They all have them nowadays. The wife wants me to grow one 'and look like an old-fashioned Player's cigarette?' I asked her. No, thank you."

"And grey flannel trousers under his white jacket."

"If you'd been among these cruisers, as they call them, as long as I have, you wouldn't be surprised if she'd seen purple tights, sir. She might have imagined anything."

"She might. But she didn't. She saw very clearly a man in a white jacket and grey flannel trousers coming into her cabin in which he expected to find someone else."

Leacock laughed aloud, "Well, I don't suppose he expected to find her, if what the steward says she's like is true."

"The cabin had been allotted to a Mr and Mrs Darwin. It was a double cabin—number forty-six. Mr Darwin could not leave his business in time and is joining the ship in Lisbon. So the occupants of the cabin were changed. This might account for the intruder's surprise on finding Mrs Grahame-Willows there."

"Of course I know nothing about that," said Leacock, "I don't have anything to do with the cabins. My job's on deck. What I thought you wanted to see me about, when the Captain told me that you were a sort of detective, was this business the night before last."

"I was more interested in the intruder, to tell you the truth."

Leacock laughed again.

"We get those every trip," he said. "Whenever there's women travelling alone."

"So you've said."

"Now that fellow the night before last was something unusual. Asleep in the saloon when everyone else had gone to bed. What do you make of that?"

"I don't," said Carolus.

"I mean, it gave me quite a start. I've known drunks lying about the ship, but this fellow wasn't drunk. Not by any means."

"How do you know?"

"I could see him, couldn't I?"

"Could you? What did he look like?"

It seemed that Leacock did not much care for the question.

"Sort of . . . ordinary," he said. "Like you might see every day."

"I thought you said he was unusual?"

"I said finding him there was unusual."

"What height would you say he was?"

"About my height, I should say. Five foot eleven, that is."

"No beard?"

"No. Nothing on his face at all. Clean shaven, like me."

"That's not so usual nowadays. How was he dressed?"

"Can't say I noticed. Or if I did I don't remember. There can't have been anything very striking about him, can there?"

"Was he wearing a raincoat?"

"Now you come to mention it I think he was. The one that was found after he'd gone overboard."

"Did he wear spectacles?"

Leacock looked narrowly—or was it suspiciously?—at Carolus.

"No," he said loudly. "No, I'm sure he wasn't. But he might have taken them off, mightn't he? You never know. Remember, he'd just been woken up."

"Yes. I do remember. You woke him, I believe?"

"Certainly I did. You can't have passengers sleeping all over the ship, can you? He ought to have been in his cabin."

"How do you know he had one? He wasn't on the passenger list."

"That's something I know nothing about. You could ask the Purser about that. As far as I know he was a passenger like any other."

"Except that from what you tell us he was on the point of committing suicide?"

"I wasn't to know that, was I? He didn't look like a man having his last minutes on earth."

"How did he look, Leacock?"

"I've told you, just ordinary."

"He didn't seem nervous?"

"Not at all. A bit sleepy if anything."

"Yet a minute or two later when you'd gone round to the other side of the saloon, he had taken his overcoat and jacket off, undone his shoes and gone over the side?"

"That's what it looked like. That's why I shouted 'Man Overboard!'"

"Do you still think that's what happened?"

"As we used to say in the Service, sir, I'm not paid to think. That's what it looked like, anyway."

"You're quite certain that you'd never seen the man before?"

"How can anyone be certain of a thing like that? For all I know we might have travelled in the same railway carriage, or something of the sort. But I don't remember it."

"You would know him again?"

"Well, not if he's gone over the side, as it seems he has. I shouldn't know him then. Have you ever seen a stiff that's been three or four days in the sea? It's not a pleasant sight I can tell you. They seem to go for their eyes first."

"There's no evidence except your own that there was such a man. He's not shown on the passenger list."

Leacock looked hostile and defiant.

"I saw him, all right," he said.

"But you didn't see him go over the side?"

"Not see him in the act, I didn't. But when a man's there one minute and the next he's gone and his coat and shoes are all that's left of him, you can pretty well tell what's happened, can't you?"

"No," said Carolus.

"Well, all I can say is, if you'll excuse me, you can't be much of a detective. I should have thought it was obvious."

"It was. Too obvious. At least that could be the explanation. It could have been what you were meant to think." Carolus paused. "Or it could not, of course. Another thing, Leacock. Do you remember Mrs Travers?"

"Mrs Travers? You mean Mrs Darwin, surely?"

"No. I meant Mrs Travers. Do you remember her on the ship about a year ago?"

Leacock grinned.

"I should think I do. Quite a bit of talk it caused."

"What caused?"

"We get used to that sort of thing. Nothing out of the way on these cruises. But there it was—her old man out of the way and her running round with this Darwin fellow. No wonder they had to get married. If you'd been on board at the time you'd have seen it coming."

"Indeed."

"You say he's joining us at Lisbon. That'll be a funny turn-out."

"You think so?"

"No worse than any of the others. Look at that Lady Spittals. Call her a lady?"

"Don't you?"

"Well, it depends what you mean by a lady. If it's being a lady to meet the Second Engineer every night when her old man's gone to bed, I suppose she is one. But it's not what I've been brought up to think a lady is. Then there's that blonde. You must have seen her. One of the last to come on board."

It was evident that Leacock had found a topic after his own heart.

"What about her?" asked Carolus innocently.

"What about her? Well the Mate's had it off with her already and the Chief Steward's got his eye on her, too. I mean to say. I'm not saying she's not all right. I daresay she is for anyone who likes that type. Only you can tell what she comes on a cruise for, can't you?"

Leacock laughed boisterously.

"Isn't she with a young man? A passenger?"

"That's what he was hoping. Not a chance when this lot they call officers got their eyes on her. And have you seen that thin piece of goods? Rabbit-mouthed sort. I saw you talking to her the first day out. Fancy her, do you?"

Carolus did not answer. Anything he could say would sound unbearably priggish.

"I thought you did," said Leacock. "Noticed right away. We shall be in to Lisbon the day after tomorrow so you'll be able to take her ashore."

"When do we get in?"

"Tomorrow night. Into the Tagus, that is. We come in and lie outside the port till daylight."

"How do you know all this?"

"Regular every trip. So many hours out from Southampton.
Up the Tagus overnight, then in to the docks for you lot to go
ashore. Though what you find to do all day I can't imagine. I
always wait till we get to Tunis where you can enjoy yourself.
But that's how it is every trip. Never varies. Anyway, I wish
you luck with that tall thin one. Not my type, but I daresay it
suits you. Now if you was to say the blonde it would be different."

"Thank you, Leacock. I think you've given me all the information I wanted."

"Glad to oblige. I don't know what you're trying to find
out but anyway . . . Cheerio, then. See you on deck some
time."

Leacock lumbered out and Carolus decided to get some
fresh air.

He was amused to see Mr Gorringer being an Edwardian
escort to Mrs Darwin. They were pacing the deck side by side
and in seemingly deep conversation.

"Do you know Mrs Darwin?" the headmaster called to
Carolus. "My former history master, Carolus Deene," he explained.

"We have met," said Mrs Darwin, without any great
warmth.

"Mrs Darwin had been telling me that she will be joined
by her husband in the port of Lisbon," went on Mr Gorringer.
"He is flying out from England while we plough our way
through the sea. What an age we live in!"

"Guy likes flying," Mrs Darwin explained. "He was in
the Royal Air Force during the war."

"Indeed? A splendid service. My own unhappy lot was to
be prevented by duty from taking part in actual combat. I was
however one of that often derided faction, the Home Guard.

Memorable days for me! Your husband will complete the cruise
with us, I trust?"

"I expect so. But you never know with Guy. He goes flying off when you least expect it."

"Ah, yes. These business tycoons. I know something of
their ways. Here today, on an aeroplane bound for New York
tomorrow. But I assure you, dear Mrs Darwin, that whatever
your husband's movements you will not be left unescorted on
this ship. I shall consider it my pleasurable duty to look after
you. Ah, I see Lady Spittals approaching with her usual smile.
She is indeed the very life and soul of the ship, is she not?"

"Hullo!" called Lady Spittals. "Win anything in the
sweepstake on the ship's run this morning?"

"I fear not," said Mr Gorringer. "Did Fortune treat you
any better?"

"Yes. I won a fiver. Not bad, was it? Of course Lazybones
wouldn't bother to buy a ticket. That's Sir Charles. Couldn't
leave his book, I suppose."

"Yes. I've noticed that Sir Charles Spittals is a great reader."

"Great reader! He can't hardly take his eyes off the page.
I tell him, aren't you coming down to see the film?, I say. But
he won't budge. As for dancing . . ."

"There you touch on a tender spot, Lady Spittals. I myself
am a notable failure in that respect. I am willing enough, even
anxious to assist, but fear that my clumsiness would cause
embarrassment to a partner."

"It's a good thing you know it, that's all," said Lady
Spittals. "Half of them don't. Have you put your name down
for the deck tennis, though?"

"Oh yes, indeed. I feel we should essay every sport even
though we have no experience. I trust you have done the same,
Deene?"

But Carolus seemed to be interested in something far out at sea, and did not answer.

———

He was however, fully awake during the following night when, as if drawn by those curious instincts of his, he pulled on his clothes and left his cabin. The group he found outside the Purser's office had much in common with the trio he had found on deck on the first night out. The Captain was there and Mr Porteous but instead of the deck-hand Leacock, Carolus found the Purser and Dr Yaqub Ali. They were talking not excitedly but with quiet seriousness.

The doctor said: "There is no doubt, I'm afraid, that it was murder."

Mr Porteous said "Oh God!" but Carolus coolly asked *what* was murder.

"An unfortunate lady passenger," said the doctor. "A Mrs Darwin. Some considerable violence was used."

"Knife? Club? Or strangled?"

"Strangled, apparently. I haven't been able to make a definite decision but I think there is no doubt."

"Wasn't her door locked?" asked Carolus.

It was the Purser who answered.

"No, Mr Deene," he said.

"Why not?"

"It was not wished to alarm the cruisers. If we had issued general instructions it would certainly have caused alarm. For many of them it would have spoilt their holiday."

"It might have saved a woman's life," said Carolus. Then perhaps recalling Leacock's account of single women on a holiday cruise, he added, "Unless she opened the door of her own accord."

This seemed to cheer Mr Porteous.

"You think she may have done?"

Carolus could not answer in Leacock's words because he *was,* in fact, paid to think.

"It's a possibility," he said.

"She has seemed rather friendly with one of the passengers," said the Purser, "though I have no idea whether that has anything to do with it. She was sitting in the saloon with him all yesterday evening, a Mr Gorringer."

Carolus turned on him.

"Don't be a fool, Ratchett," he said. "They were playing Scrabble."

As though to relieve the tension the doctor said, "Scrabble? What on earth is that?"

Someone answered rather contemptuously. "It's a game." Then the Purser said, speaking directly to the Captain, "I have locked the door, sir. I think we may leave things as they are until the morning."

"And in the morning?" Carolus asked, "what do you intend to do? Report it to the Port Authorities?"

Porteous answered him.

"No need for that at all. The doctor is quite uncertain of the manner of the woman's death. There may even be some uncertainty about whether she *is* dead. Isn't that so, Dr Yaqub Ali?" He hurried on before the doctor could answer. "There is no need to report it to anyone. The lady is indisposed—in her cabin."

"You can't get away with this, Porteous," Carolus said. "It wasn't certain that a man was overboard. It is quite certain that a woman has been killed."

Porteous began, "Let's say, for the sake of argument . . ."

"There's no argument," said Carolus.

"What you should be concerned with, Mr Deene," said Porteous, "is the identity of the murderer. You can safely leave

the matter of reporting this occurrence to the Captain and
me. Have you any idea what it would mean if we reported it?
Half the Portuguese police on board, the ship not allowed to
leave port, the passengers cross-examined, their holidays completely spoilt . . . After all, you undertook to do your best to
prevent anything like this happening. It is up to you to clear
up the mystery, not to go running to the police of a foreign
country. This is a British ship."

Carolus turned sharply away.

But before he went to his cabin he said, "There's one thing
you're overlooking. The woman's husband is due to come on
board today. What are you going to tell him?"

Like Pontius Pilate, he did not wait for an answer.

Six

THE FIRST MAN CAROLUS sought in the morning was the Purser. He avoided Mr Gorringer taking his before-breakfast stroll on deck, did not go in to breakfast, and found the Purser in his cabin.

"I don't think Porteous and Scorer have the ghost of a chance of getting away with this," he said. "But that will be their funeral. I want to know whether anyone came on board last night."

Mr Ratchett nodded. "I thought you were going to ask that," he said. "Yes, quite unexpectedly at around one o'clock. A clerk from the agent's office."

"Name?" queried Carolus.

"Costa Neves. We know him well. He comes on board as a matter of course, but I've never known him do so on the night we lay off in the Tagus. We're usually alongside by nine o'clock in the morning and he comes on then."

"What brought him out to the ship?"

"The usual documents. But they could have been attended to this morning."

"How did he come out?"

"In the agent's launch."

"So you lowered the gangplank?"

"Yes. Costa Neves is a little lame."

53

"Was anyone in the launch with him?"

"Only the two boatmen who are always with the launch. I know them both."

"Surely you could not identify them in the dark from on deck, Mr Ratchett?"

"Near enough. I know the two, you see."

"You mean that because you know the boatmen usually with the launch, you assumed that these were the two?"

"I suppose that was it. But since Costa Neves said nothing, it was a pretty safe assumption."

"Leaving the possibility that the launch brought almost anyone out to the ship?"

"Why should it? I know Costa Neves. See him every trip."

"Does he know any of the passengers?"

"Oh, I shouldn't think so. He only speaks a little English and when he comes aboard he's usually pretty busy. Why? You're not suggesting he killed Mrs Darwin?"

"No. But he could have. Or someone he brought aboard with him."

"He brought no one aboard. I watched him come up the gangplank. He and the two boatmen came alone in the launch. And for the whole time the launch was alongside there was a man at the top of the gangplank."

"Which man?"

"Leacock. He's our most reliable deckhand."

"I'm not entirely satisfied with that. But let it pass for the moment. Who occupied the cabin next to Mrs Darwin?"

"Sir Charles and Lady Spittals."

"And opposite?"

"Miss Berry."

"I intend to interview them. If they ask me questions I shall tell them the truth. I won't be part of what I consider a conspiracy."

Yet a few minutes later, when Carolus met Mr Gorringer coming up from the dining room, he found himself—while not actually lying—at least not going out of his way to proclaim the truth.

"I hear that our friend Mrs Darwin is not well this morning," Mr Gorringer said. "I had hoped to escort her ashore to show her some of the sights of the capital of our oldest ally."

"Pity. I'm afraid you'll have to go alone. Unless you care to invite Miss Berry."

"My dear Deene, far be it from me to appear to be in the least critical of one of our fellow-passengers, but I have noticed the lady you mention seeming somewhat eager in her approach to the male sex. I might find her an embarrassment."

"Yes. You might. I have work to do this morning. Have a good time ashore."

The headmaster seemed distinctly put out when Carolus left him, but this passed, for a few moments later Mr Gorringer could be seen greeting several other passengers heartily, as they made their way towards the dock gates.

Meanwhile Carolus was just in time to catch Sir Charles and Lady Spittals dressed ready to go ashore but delayed by the unwillingness of Sir Charles to leave the saloon.

"You go, dear," the ex-Lord Mayor said after they had both greeted Carolus.

"Isn't that just like him?" Lady Spittals demanded of Carolus, or of the world in general. "We've booked a nice expedition with some of the cruisers and he says 'you go' as though I wanted to get off with someone. It's always 'you go' with him. I don't know why he bothers to get up in the morning at all."

"I was going to ask you whether you would be so good as to answer a few questions," Carolus said tentatively. "About last night."

"That poor thing!" said Lady Spittals. She at once sat down and seemed to forget the expedition ashore, attracted by this new and exciting topic. "It's true, then? She was murdered?"

"True or not," said Carolus evasively, "I think you're more likely to know what happened than anyone."

"Me? I don't know what you mean."

"Mr Deene is reminding us that we were in the cabin next door," said Sir Charles. "Wasn't that it, Mr Deene?"

"Yes. I thought you were bound to hear something."

"Not a sound," said Lady Spittals. "That's why we couldn't believe it when we heard this morning what had happened."

"What did you hear?"

"About these men coming out in a yacht and murdering Mrs Darwin. At least that's what we were told. It seems they were some kind of Arabs."

"Cypriots, didn't the lady say?" suggested Sir Charles.

"Or was it the I.R.A.? One of those lots anyhow. But they must have been silent doing it because we never heard a murmur. Why should they have picked on her, I wonder? She seemed quite a harmless sort of woman. Not what you'd call a ball of fire but not one you'd think would get her throat cut like that."

"I thought we were told she was smothered?" said Sir Charles.

"What does it matter? She was murdered, anyway. And to think we slept right through it all."

"You didn't hear any voices?"

"No. Of course the engines make some noise. Perhaps that's what drowned it."

Just then another woman hurried up to them.

"Come along, you two!" she said excitedly. "We're all waiting!"

"He doesn't want to come," said Lady Spittals, not bitterly but apparently with amusement. "He says, 'You go,

dear'"—and just then Sir Charles said it. Indeed, what else
was there to say?

"All right, I will!" said Lady Spittals defiantly. "And I hope
you enjoy yourself sitting there all day. Come on, Mrs Popple."

The two hurried out, leaving Sir Charles with a look of
something like contentment on his face.

"Steward!" he called with unexpected vigour, and to Carolus, "Will you have a drink? I know it's a bit early, but I could
do with one."

Carolus agreed.

It was while the steward was bringing their drinks that
Carolus became aware of a curious sniffing noise behind him
and, turning round, saw Miss Berry, with red eyes and a sod-
den handkerchief. He swallowed his whisky and went across
to her. He was not very good at situations like this. Did one
say "Now, now" or "This won't do, will it?" He went for a
simple question.

"What's the matter?" he asked.

She shook her head.

"Have a drink?" tried Carolus.

"A whisky, please. Without ice and just a splash of soda."

The "splash" was too much for her, it seemed, and after
giving these precise instructions she started to weep again,
rather noisily.

"Upset about Mrs Darwin?" Carolus asked.

Miss Berry looked at him with astonishment.

"Mrs Darwin?" she spluttered. "What's she done? It's not
her."

"There is a story going round the ship," said Carolus with
literal truth but far from candid intent, "that she was murdered."

Miss Berry digested that. But it did nothing to calm her
tears.

"I don't care if she was. She said last night I looked off-colour and offered me some liver salts. I could have murdered her myself."

"But you didn't? Then why are you crying?"

"It's not Mrs Darwin. It's Gavin Ritchie."

Carolus recognized the name of the good-looking but rather sullen young man he had seen coming aboard.

"What's he done?"

"He was all right yesterday. We were together nearly all the evening. He promised to take me ashore today to see . . ." Miss Berry broke down again. "To see the fish market," she said finally.

Well, that's a new one, thought Carolus, but did not say it.

"What do you care about a lot of old fish?" He knew it was no good as soon as he said it. Miss Berry cried again.

"Not the fish," she explained. "It's the women. They carry the baskets on their heads. Gavin wanted to see that. He's an artist, you know. Now he's gone ashore with the Assistant Purser who looks like a girl."

"Surely you don't care about that?"

"I do. I care terribly. I thought at last, when I met Gavin, that this was going to be a wonderful cruise."

"Perhaps it is. I want to ask you something. Miss Berry . . ."

"Susan."

"I wanted to ask you, Susan, whether you heard anything unusual in the night. Your cabin's opposite to Mrs Darwin's."

"I don't know what you mean by unusual," said Susan, who had grown suddenly sour. "I suppose it's not unusual on this ship to hear knocking on the cabin door of a woman passenger when she's supposed to be alone."

"Yours?" asked Carolus, unable to suppress a suggestion of incredulity.

"No. Not mine. I wouldn't have it. On Mrs Darwin's door."

"You heard that? At what time?"

"Some time after one, it must have been, because I didn't go to bed till nearly one and was reading for a long time."

"If I may ask you, Susan, where were you between, say, midnight and one o'clock?"

"Of course you may. I don't care any more. I was with Gavin."

"Did you see a launch come alongside?"

"Some kind of a boat, yes. I didn't really notice much about it. I wasn't particularly interested, to tell the truth. Anyway. It was just before I went to bed because Gavin said we had to be up early in the morning to see the . . ."

"Yes. I know. The fish market. So you didn't wait to see whether anyone came aboard from the launch?"

"No. I went to my cabin."

"And some time afterwards you heard someone knocking at Mrs Darwin's door?"

"Yes. But before that I heard a noise in the passage. The young Dunlearys were laughing and running about."

"You didn't look out to see who it was who knocked?"

Susan Berry hesitated, then said, "Well, I did just want to see that it wasn't anyone I knew. So I peeped out. But whoever it was had gone into Mrs Darwin's cabin and shut the door. So I went to bed. I didn't think anything more about it."

"And you didn't hear any more?"

"No. The first thing I heard was in the morning when I went into breakfast. Someone was saying there had been a murder, but I was waiting for Gavin to come down. He sits at the same table and he's usually pretty cheerful at breakfast. But when he came, he scarcely spoke a word for a long time. Then he told me he had to do some shopping ashore so he was going with the Assistant Purser who knew all the ropes. That was all he said and I watched them going off the ship together. Then you came up and started asking me questions."

"I'm sorry if I annoyed you."

"Oh, no. You didn't. It was just that I thought Gavin was going to be a real friend . . ."

"Just one question more," Carolus said. "Had you ever heard anyone knock at Mrs Darwin's door in the night before last night?"

"Well, there may have been. You know what this ship is—"

"But you hadn't heard it?"

"Not to be certain of."

"You think you may have?"

"Oh, I don't know," cried Susan, losing all patience. "No one knocked on *my* door, I know that."

Carolus called the steward and ordered two more drinks.

"Who is the young officer who has just come in?" he asked Susan.

She seemed to recover at once.

"Which? Where?" she asked.

"I think it's the Second Engineer."

Susan appeared transfixed.

"Yes," she said. "I thought he'd gone ashore, too. Do you mind if I go out on deck? It's rather stuffy in here."

As she left him Carolus caught a glimpse of Leacock with a broad and meaningful grin on his face peering in from the deck. He remembered what the man had said and felt just a little embarrassed.

Sir Charles Spittals was signalling to him to rejoin him.

"Just time for another," he said. "They're coming back for lunch, you see. The ship sails at two. What's it going to be?"

Carolus refused, and went out on deck. He was anxious to know whether Mrs Darwin's, the *late* Mrs Darwin's, husband had arrived as promised.

Susan Berry's mention of the young Dunlearys had reminded him of the fact, so disturbing to Mr Porteous, that the
family from County Dublin were very much in evidence at
times. Perhaps because they, like most Irish families, had a
clutch of children, he had simply put them out of his mind. He
admitted this was illogical, but he found it impossible to connect them with anything more sinister than singing "The Wearing of the Green" at a ship's concert.

Seven

AFTER LUNCH MRS STICK called Carolus into the Sun Lounge with an air of urgency.

"You've got your murder all right then, sir," she whispered, though there seemed to be no one within earshot. "I told you, you would have. That poor thing whose husband died on this very ship last year."

"Are you sure about it, Mrs Stick?

"Sure? Of course I'm sure. The lady at the table where we sit knew all about it at breakfast time this morning, only I couldn't find you to tell you."

"I thought perhaps she might. Did she say how she heard?"

"There's not much she doesn't hear, if you ask me," said Mrs Stick. "She was told it was two of the crew done it, battering the poor lady something cruel. It just shows you, doesn't it? What can happen when you come on a cruise like this. As I said this morning, I said, 'They're all smiles when they see you walking about but you never know what they're planning among themselves,' Look at what happened to her, I mean."

This was altogether too allusive for Carolus.

"To whom?" he asked politely.

"The lady at the table where we sit. I told you how one of the stewards tried to get into her cabin."

"You told me nothing of the sort. You expressly said the man who came to her cabin at night was not a steward. He had grey flannel trousers."

"It's all the same when you're in bed and they come in after you. Anyway, this time it happened to poor Mrs Darwin and she's not alive to tell the tale."

"But her husband is," said Carolus. "And I rather think he will tell it with some force. He's due on board any minute now. His plane must have come down nearly an hour ago."

Mrs Stick looked rather awed and said nothing.

"Didn't the lady at the table where you sit know that?" Carolus asked with a touch of banter.

"She didn't happen to mention it at lunch," replied Mrs Stick airily. "She was talking about the young lady who was taken to the fish market this morning, Miss Berry her name is, and got left there, trying to find her way out, and was shouted at by all the Portuguese women walking about with fish on their heads. They say poor Miss Berry came on board smelling something dreadful of fish, and I suppose you can't wonder, really."

Carolus was stung into a retort.

"That whole story is untrue," he said. "Miss Berry was left on board this morning and was talking to me. She wanted to see the fish market but never got there."

Mrs Stick sniffed. It was evident that she preferred her own authority to Carolus's.

"That's what the lady at the table where we sit said, anyway," she stated with finality.

The steward in charge of the Sun Lounge approached and told Carolus that the Captain would like to see him in his cabin, so he left Mrs Stick and followed the steward's directions.

He found Captain Scorer with Mr Porteous and the Purser, but this time there was a stranger with them, a clean and spruce-looking man in his early fifties.

"Let me introduce Mr Deene. Mr Darwin," said the Captain.

Darwin seemed calm, though Carolus thought at once that it was the habitual manner of a man who did not exhibit his emotions, though he might be feeling great distress. He nodded to Carolus and, after an awkward silence, Porteous, addressing Carolus, said, "We have been breaking our tragic news to Mr Darwin."

"I hope you have told him the truth," said Carolus.

"What truth?" Darwin almost shouted.

"The truth that last night, Mr Darwin, your wife was murdered."

A cry broke from Darwin but he did not speak.

"I wished to break this as gently as possible to Mr Darwin," said Porteous reproachfully.

"No purpose can be served by leaving Mr Darwin to discover for himself from ship's gossip. I'm sure we all express our deepest sympathy, Mr Darwin, but you had better know the truth."

Then Darwin turned to Porteous and asked in a quiet strained voice, "When you received these threatening letters, just what precautions did you take?"

Porteous cleared his throat.

"You will understand that the happiness of a large number of people is my responsibility. I did not wish to alarm them. The letters might be a fake or the act of a madman . . ."

"In that case was there not all the more need to take measures for the protection of your passengers?"

"Cruisers," corrected Mr Porteous. "Of course there was, and we took those measures. I employed Carolus Deene, a well-known investigator."

For the first time Darwin showed some emotion. It was anger.

"What the hell is the good of an investigator after it has happened?" he asked. "You needed an armed policeman, not an amateur detective. I mean no disrespect to Mr Deene, of course. But events, tragic events as I understand them, have shown that I am right."

"I agree entirely," said Carolus. "I should never have been asked to act as a security guard. But I'm afraid you're wrong in talking of an armed policeman. It would have been totally impracticable to try that sort of thing to protect every passenger."

"Was there nothing in these letters to suggest that it was my wife who was in danger?"

"Nothing. Had there been you would have been told at once."

"In that case I should never have let her come out here alone, whatever the cost to my business."

"What is your business. Mr Darwin?" asked Carolus.

Darwin answered with a single word which seemed to say all that was necessary.

"Property."

"What the Americans call Real Estate?"

"Exactly. I had to be in London yesterday for a most important meeting. But of course if I had been given the smallest indication that my wife was threatened, I should not have let her come."

"You did not receive any letters of a type similar to those Mr Porteous had?" Carolus asked.

"None."

"Tell me, Mr Darwin. Have you ever heard the name Alexander Carlisle?"

Darwin hesitated.

"In what connection?"

"In any connection. Property, perhaps? Or just something personal?"

"There is a familiar ring about the name," said Mr Darwin. "Does he appear on television?"

"I have no idea. But he's on this ship. A Jamaican."

"I see."

Did he? Carolus wondered.

But Darwin was talking again.

"I suppose you have done right not to inform the Portuguese authorities. I certainly don't want my poor wife's body taken away to some morgue. But aren't you taking a certain risk in not informing them of a thing of this kind?"

Both Porteous and Scorer nodded solemnly.

"Undoubtedly," Porteous said. "But it seemed to us that the decision should be left to you."

"I appreciate that. The decision, if you like, but not the responsibility. I can't relieve you of that. I can only say that I would prefer that my wife's body should be taken to England for burial. A cremation. You must decide whether you can carry out my wishes."

"Do you plan to accompany us?" asked Porteous.

"You mean on a pleasure cruise?" asked Darwin impatiently.

"I realize, of course, that it can be no such thing for you. But I thought perhaps you might wish to remain with your wife's body."

"That was thoughtful of you. I am, as you must all understand, too shocked at the moment to decide. If I had not been met this morning at the airport and warned of what to expect when I came on board, I should have had no inkling."

"Who met you?" asked Porteous rather sharply.

"A Señor Costa Neves."

The Purser intervened. "I arranged that. I felt that it should not be broken suddenly to Mr Darwin."

"Thank you," said Darwin. He looked pale and wretched. "But as Mr Deene says, no purpose is served by concealing the truth from me. Have you any suspicions about it yet? I mean, suspicions of anyone connected with it?"

"None worth formulating," said Carolus. "But I mean to know who murdered your wife, Mr Darwin. Also exactly how and why. I shall report first to you when I have anything more than remote guesswork."

"How—please don't try to spare any feelings—how was it done?"

"Your wife, according to the ship's doctor, was probably strangled," said Carolus.

"Probably? Doesn't he *know*?"

"Again," said Porteous, "we have awaited your arrival to make a detailed examination."

"Then please wait no longer," said Darwin curtly. "We must have the maximum information and as soon as possible."

Carolus found this cool, though evidently troubled, man surprising but in the circumstances welcome. He had imagined a husband more outraged than grief-stricken, abusing everyone connected with the ship and her ill-fated cruise. He began to understand what Ratchett had meant when he spoke of a charming fellow.

"Do you wish to go down to your wife's cabin?" asked the Purser in the tones of an undertaker consulting the wishes of "the family."

"Of course. Before the doctor makes his examination."

"Then I will take you down myself," said Ratchett. "We all feel the deepest sympathy."

Darwin turned to Carolus. "Later I should be glad if we could have a talk," he said. Again Carolus felt grateful to him for not speaking of "a few words" as Mr Gorringer surely would have done.

"Certainly. Meet you in the Bar Lounge in half an hour's time," he offered.

Darwin nodded and followed the Purser to the door. But he turned back.

"I take it you have examined my wife's body?" he said to Carolus.

"No. Not much in my line, I'm afraid. I've never learnt anything from a cadaver that was not in the doctor's report. And I don't think the puzzle of this crime will be solved by a microscope or any other of the forensic aids."

"Really?" Porteous intervened, sounding rather hostile. "Then how do you expect to solve it, Mr Deene?"

"Common sense and perhaps a touch of instinct—for want of a better word."

Darwin scarcely waited to hear this.

"I hope you're not depending too much on instinct," said Porteous.

"I don't think so. I'll find out who killed Cynthia Darwin, anyway."

"Have you in the meantime found out who was responsible for the threatening letters?"

"I have a pretty good idea. I know who it *wasn't* and that's half the battle."

"No doubt you will inform me, in that case?"

"All in good time," said Carolus.

Darwin was waiting for him at a table in a far corner of the saloon called the Bar Lounge.

"I've seen my wife," he said. "Seems pretty certain she was strangled. That accords with the fact that the passengers in the next cabin, so the Purser tells me, heard nothing at all."

"Did the Purser tell you what the girl in the cabin opposite heard?"

Darwin stared.

"No. What?" he asked.

"Not a very reliable witness, I'm afraid. One of the saddest good-time girls I have known. She says she heard someone knocking on the door of your wife's cabin. She looked out but by the time she did so the man or woman had entered the cabin and closed the door."

"I should have said 'impossible' an hour ago. I have learned better than to say that of anything. But I certainly can't account for it. She surely could not have invited anyone to come to her cabin at one or two in the morning. Unless . . ."

"Unless what, Mr Darwin?"

"I was going to say unless she asked one of the women passengers. For company or something."

"In that case it would suggest that she was strangled by a woman. Not very likely, I should have thought."

"Not necessarily. She might have expected a woman and left her door unlocked. The woman might have introduced a man."

"Needless to say I have gone over the possibilities in my mind," said Carolus. "Including the possibility that Sir Charles and Lady Spittals, or Miss Berry, the girl in the cabin opposite, are lying. Or that one of them is.

"But you've reached no conclusion?"

"No. I haven't. No final conclusion."

"To you this is just a puzzling case," said Darwin rather sadly. "To me it is the loss of my wife. We had only been married six months."

"So I understand."

"Did you meet her?"

"Just for a few moments when she first came on board."

"I was deeply in love with her," said Darwin. "I'm sure you appreciate that. I am as determined as you are to discover the truth. Meanwhile I have had time to consider the practical side of the situation. I shall ask Porteous and the Captain if the ship can put in at Gibraltar before entering the Mediterranean instead of on its way back to England. Then I shall pay for a special flight to carry her body home and I shall go with it. I should think Porteous would be more than ready for the sake of the other passengers. It must all be an embarrassment to him."

"I suppose so. He's always speaking of his responsibility for the happiness of his cruisers. I think, if I may say so, that your plan is a good one."

"In this way there will be a proper postmortem."

Carolus looked keenly at him.

"Most people, when they lose a relative, are horrified by the idea. I'm glad you see it in that light."

It will cost a lot of money," said Darwin unexpectedly. "But I shall be glad if it only helps a little to get at the truth."

"Yes. I see that."

"But you have no idea, even a sheer guess, where the truth lies?"

"I wouldn't say that. We all indulge in guesswork sometimes. But at present I have nothing even to form the basis of a list of possible suspects."

"Let us be hypothetical though, Deene. Who would be on that list if you decided to make it now?"

"Almost everyone on the ship, to start with. The officers and crew and all the passengers."

"*All* the passengers?"

"Why not? If you suspect one it must be all of them, men and women. But it doesn't end there. The Purser will have told you that a launch put out from the docks last night at about one o'clock. The agent's clerk, apparently. The man who met you at the airport this morning. That widens the range considerably."

"Why?"

"There were two boatmen on the launch whom Ratchett assumed to be the usual crew of the launch. But no one knows. The launch seems to have been alongside for the best part of an hour. You see why I say this widens the range of possibility?"

"You mean that the murderer might have been concealed aboard the launch?"

"Or could have been one of the men whom Ratchett took for boatmen. There are a number of possibilities. All in all, I see no point in trying to make a list of suspects at the moment. Perhaps I may be able to suggest something before you leave us at Gibraltar. You have not been concerned in any way with the troubles in Northern Ireland, I suppose?"

"I have some property there. And in the South. But surely this could have no connection?"

"I mention it only because some of the younger members of an Irish family were playing in the corridor rather noisily near your wife's cabin. Their connection seems the most far-fetched of suppositions, but since I was given the information, I pass it on to you."

"Thanks. I see your difficulties. Don't let me add to them by asking you to investigate every ridiculous piece of guess-work of the passengers."

Eight

NO ONE AMONG THE passengers on the sixty-fifth cruise of the *Summer Queen* was likely to forget the events of the night she left Lisbon for the journey down to Gibraltar, and the greatest addicts of holiday cruising swore after them that they would never go on a cruise again. The sea was rough, for one thing, and the wind and inky darkness of the night made the name of the ship, and of the company which chartered it, a mockery. But there was more to it than bad weather and Carolus himself felt, in words quoted from one of his favourite authors, that almost anything was rather more than likely to happen.

On the first night out from Lisbon, none of the officers appeared at dinner and it was said that they were all needed for their mysterious duties on the bridge or in the engine room. As Mrs Stick told Carolus after dinner, "*She* says they know it's bad luck to carry a corpse on board."

Carolus was amused to notice that reference to "the lady at the table where we sit" had become shortened at last to the simple if majuscular She, the full title being too pleonastic even for Mrs Stick who loved, as she said, to call things by their proper names.

"She says it's no wonder all the officers are needed to keep the ship from turning over when there's a dead body in one of the cabins. And look at this wind! It'll be a wonder if any of us will be alive in the morning to tell the tale. Stick says he's known some rough weather in his time but this beats it all. He says it's as though there's something unnatural about it and you can't really wonder, can you?"

Carolus tried to look sympathetic.

"Then there's that Mr Medlow, as he calls himself."

"Isn't that his name?"

"Well, it may be for all I know, but I sometimes wonder if he knows himself, the way he's carrying on. You hear of people not being all there but I don't think he knows whether he is or not, shouting the way he does.'

"Shouting?"

"You should have heard him. Running round the saloon waving his walking stick and saying 'Where's Porteous? Where's Porteous? I'm going to kill that bastard!'"

"Perhaps he'd had a drink too many."

"I don't know what he'd had but it upsets anyone when they're having a quiet chat to have someone shouting like that. Then She has to say, 'He will, too. He means it,' which only shows how some people take anything like that. Of course you've heard about Lady Spittals, haven't you? That's another thing. All her jewellery gone!"

"But I've just been speaking to her. She was wearing quite a lot of it."

"That's what She told me. She said no sooner had Lady Spittals gone to her cabin to get ready for dinner when she knew someone had been there. Sort of sensed it, She said, and when she came to look in her jewel box it was empty, so she rang for the steward, She said, and when he came he looked ever so funny as though he'd got something to hide, so she knew what it was and went straight to the Purser and told him all about it. If you say she was wearing it when she was with you she must of got it back then, mustn't she?"

"We'll soon find out," said Carolus, and went across to
Lady Spittals.

"I've just heard a story that you've lost some jewellery,"
he said.

"Well, if that doesn't take the cake I don't know what
does," said Lady Spittals. "All that happened was that when I
went down to our cabin this evening, I had a feeling that someone had been there. You know that feeling, when someone's
just left a room? I'm very quick to feel anything like that. I can
always tell if there's a cat in the room, for instance. Mother
used to say I had second sight. So tonight I just felt it. A stranger
I mean, not Charles or the cabin steward. But all that about
jewellery's so much nonsense. I keep most of it in the ship's
safe, anyway. These are just a few little things I happen to
have with me." She indicated a display of brilliants which reminded Carolus of the Tower of London.

"I'm so glad you haven't lost anything. It was just alarmist talk," said Carolus.

"But I'll tell you what isn't alarmist talk," said Lady
Spittals. "Because my husband himself saw it and he's the last
man to make up anything like that. It was about this strange
man on deck."

"Which one?" asked Carolus.

"You can find it funny, Mr Deene, but when Charles tells
me something I know it's true. He saw this man coming up
the stairs from the lower part—where the children play in the
daytime. Only it was dark when he saw him."

"Then, you mustn't mind my asking this, how did Sir
Charles know there was anything strange about him?"

"The eyes, for one thing. Like fire, Charles says."

"But could he see them in the dark?"

"Of course he could. Charles has got eyes like a cat and he
doesn't exaggerate. Then the man was muttering to himself.
Charles couldn't catch the words but it was more like someone

in pain, he says. Charles watched him walk the whole length of the deck, then disappear. Charles said it was uncanny. He was all in black, too, and wore a hood over his head."

"A sou'wester."

"I don't know anything about that, but Charles said there was something horrible about him."

"One of the deckhands going on duty, I should think."

"Well you may, but I don't. What was he muttering about? No, you can't laugh this off, Mr Deene. There's something queer about this ship and you know it. Ask Mrs Grahame-Willows. She'll tell you."

"She seems to be an authority," said Carolus.

"It's just that she keeps her eyes open and won't be taken in by all this talk of there being nothing wrong. If there's nothing wrong why was Mrs Darwin murdered?"

"That is what I'm endeavouring to find out. But I'm not helped by sensational stories. We only need to sight the *Flying Dutchman* with all her lights blazing, running against the wind."

"Please stop that, Mr Deene. We've quite enough to upset us as it is. I hear the Captain's had a stroke from all the worry."

"I suppose Mrs Grahame-Willows told you that, too?"

"As a matter of fact she did. But that's no reason to doubt it. With a dead body on the ship, as any seaman will tell you, there are bound to be strange happenings. I advise you not to go out on deck, Mr Deene. However sceptical you are, there are dangers about tonight."

Carolus had not had the least intention of going out on deck, but the silly woman had given him a challenge and, having put on a heavy overcoat, he went out to the covered part of the deck. At first he thought he was alone, but as he passed along the row of deck chairs he saw that one of them was occupied. As he approached, he recognized Alexander Carlisle and took the deck chair next to him.

"Good evening," said the West Indian civilly. "Come out for a breather?"

He spoke in a pleasantly cultured voice.

"Yes. I'm rather sick of the old wives' tales going round the ship."

He could hear a chuckle from his companion in the darkness beside him.

"You can't really be surprised at that. They come on one of these ridiculous cruises in the hope of sunshine and all they get is a murder and foul weather."

"There's no certainty about the murder," said Carolus.

"Isn't there?" said the voice beside him in the near-darkness. The man spoke with scorn, as though Carolus was an ass to have any doubt at all. Then he added, "Mrs Darwin was murdered, all right."

"What makes you so certain about it?"

"I know," said Alexander Carlisle, as though that settled the matter for good.

"I think I've heard your name before," Carolus said, inviting confidence.

"Quite likely. I'm considered a rather dangerous man, I believe."

"If I remember correctly," said Carolus, recalling headlines, "you were up at Oxford? President of the Union?"

Again that deep chuckle.

"Does that make me dangerous?"

"Not necessarily. But I wouldn't trust you alone with our Mr Porteous for instance."

"No? You'd be wrong there. Porteous is just a figurehead. I'm more interested in those guilty of specific acts—however ignorant they may be."

"What kind of acts?"

"Oh, just acts. I work alone, Mr Deene. I don't belong to any movement or party. But I think I can make myself felt."

"Why are you telling me all this?"

"You're a private detective, aren't you? Employed by Porteous." He chuckled again. "I'm trying to help you"

"Thanks."

"But don't push your luck."

"What on earth do you mean?"

"A worm can turn, remember. Sometimes before you can tread on it."

"You know, Mr Carlisle, I think this is one of the most pointless conversations I've ever had. Certainly on a ship's deck in semi-darkness at eleven o'clock on a dirty night. Don't you?"

"Not altogether."

"But tell me something else. What brought you on this ridiculous cruise, as you call it?"

"Shall we say curiosity?"

"That's a motive I can well understand. It was partly my own. But I think it was more than that."

"Perhaps I wanted the sunshine, too."

"Perhaps. Did you know either of the Darwins before you came aboard?"

"Not personally."

"What does that mean?"

They were interrupted by some angry shouting that seemed to come from the lower well deck. Carolus at once recognized Leacock's voice raised in drunken fury. Between his four-lettered outbursts there was silence as though someone with him was trying to quieten him in softer tones. He went along to look down but in the darkness he could distinguish only Leacock. Before he had reached him whoever had been with him had gone.

Leacock was certainly drunk.

"Who were you shouting at?" Carolus asked him.

"Mind your own bloody business."

Carolus, in the course of his numerous investigations was not unaccustomed to that warning, but it had seldom been voiced with such emphasis as now.

Then Leacock said, "You ought to know. You know every bloody thing. I oughtn't to need to tell you, the lousy bastard."

"I expect I do," said Carolus. "But I'd like to hear it from you. Of course it could have been one of the officers who had found you drunk on watch . . ."

"It could have been the Queen Mother," said Leacock with a silly laugh. "But it wasn't."

On that he lurched away and when Carolus returned to the promenade deck, Alexander Carlisle had disappeared.

But Mr Gorringer, his yachting cap changed for a plaid tam-o'-shanter with a large pompom on its crown, was awaiting him.

"I wanted a word with you, Deene," he said rather gloomily. "It occurs to me that you are sometimes inclined to think that I treat with too much seriousness things that you may dismiss as trivial. You can scarcely hold me guilty of that today when we have almost been the very witnesses of a cruel and brutal murder. No one, surely, could be expected to pass that over lightly."

"Certainly not," agreed Carolus.

"Especially when the victim was a lady for whom I had already formed some esteem."

"Whoever the victim was. I never treat murder lightly."

"In that case I shall venture to make some observations. It is my fixed belief that the murderer was brought out to the ship for that very evil purpose."

"Oh. What makes you think that?"

"Are we to consider it no more than a coincidence that the agent's clerk, the man named, I understand, Costa Neves, came out in a launch at one o'clock in the small hours on that particular night when he had never done such a thing before? Was it chance that he brought two boatmen whom no one on board has been able to identify with any certainty? That the unfortunate lady met her fate during the very hour that the agent spent on this ship? Are these no more than coincidences?"

"Are you trying to tell me that you think Costa Neves was the murderer?"

"I, my dear Deene, am the merest tiro in these cases, but I do consider that the likelihood should be taken into your consideration, since we have unfortunately no professional investigator who would doubtless form his conclusions at once."

"Oh, it's taken into my consideration all right," said Carolus. "So are a thousand other possibilities. But if I were you, headmaster, I should cease to bother your"—should he say "tiny?"—"head about it. Murder will out, you know, and I already have the beginnings of a theory about this crime."

"I'm extremely glad to hear it. What an abominable night it is. Cold, dark, windy—it would seem the very elements are involved in our misfortunes. And what . . ." Mr Gorringer clutched Carolus's arm . . . "What is that?"

"That" was the sound of Miss Berry suppressing her tears. She had come from the starboard side and stood in the shadows.

"Have you seen the Second Engineer?" she asked. It was more than a question.

"No. I'm afraid not," said Carolus politely. "But Mr Gavin Ritchie is in the saloon."

"Who cares about him?" asked Miss Berry. "I want to find Douglas."

"Douglas?"

"The Second Engineer. You know him. We saw him this morning."

"If you will heed my advice, young lady," put in Mr Gorringer, "you will take what shelter and protection the ship offers you. Far be it from me to alarm you, but this is not the time to linger on deck without a trustworthy escort. You know there has been one dreadful event on this ship already."

"Oh, I don't take any notice of that," said Miss Berry. "Doesn't anybody want a good time? I thought when I booked a passage for this cruise there would be some kind of entertainment. All we've had is an out-of-date film and that silly horseracing. Not a single dance."

"You can scarcely expect passengers to be frivolous and lighthearted when they have suffered such a pitiless blow as the death of a dear and respected . . ."

"I thought you were rather gone on her," said Miss Berry. "Well, there's no accounting for taste." She turned to Carolus. "Can't you suggest where the Second Engineer might be?"

Carolus resisted the invitation to say "in the engine room," and Miss Berry returned to the shadows.

"If I were that young lady," said Mr Gorringer voicing an improbably hypothesis, "I should not wander about on deck alone."

"She doesn't want to be alone," said Carolus.

Mr Gorringer ignored this.

"Well, Deene, I have given you my views," he said. "I hope you will make what use you can of them. I will leave you to deliberate."

And that is exactly what Carolus did, for half an hour, before going to his cabin, intending to turn in. But there was one more surprise for him on that night of surprises. Sitting in the one straight armchair, studying his face in the mirror, was the man whom the Purser had described as "crackers, bark-ing, up the wall," the powerful-looking passenger named Medlow.

Carolus, as though meaning to humour him, showed no surprise at his presence.

"Hullo," he said.

Medlow made a grimace which convinced Carolus that he was acting, rather than insane.

"I know who sent those letters to Porteous," Medlow said with in apish grin.

"So do I," said Carolus coolly.

"Oh, you do. Who do you think it was?"

"You," said Carolus.

Medlow appeared taken aback. Then he decided to dis-miss it and grinned again. Finally he asked, "How did you know?"

"I've no idea what your game is," said Carolus. "But pre-tending to be soft in the head is part of it. You're at least half sane. I suppose you've got your knife into Porteous. Is that it?"

"Porteous is a cad," observed Medlow, staring into the mirror again. "A bloody racialist."

"Yes," agreed Carolus.

"He's got to learn a lesson and he will before this cruise is over. You, too. He has hired you as a watchdog. You've got it coming to you."

"Perhaps, having got that off your chest, you would be good enough to get out?"

Rather to his surprise, the big man rose to his feet and made for the door.

"Don't forget what I told you," he said. "I'd do it now, only I'm not quite ready."

Carolus sighed.

"What an incredible bore you are," he said to the broad retreating back of the other.

And now, he thought, perhaps I really can get to bed.

Nine

ON THE FOLLOWING EVENING, though the wind had gone down and the passengers seemed to have lost the look of tension that some of them had worn on the previous night, Carolus himself did not feel reassured. There was in all probability, he reminded himself, a murderer on board since, as the Purser had told him, no one had remained ashore in Lisbon, and Carolus was not the man, even among the absurdities of a holiday cruise, to treat murder lightly. As he had shown in previous cases, he had an almost superstitious awe of the very word. He was ready to see the humours of human vanity and particularly of curious idiom, but he had never found anything in the least amusing about a man or woman who usurped the authority of God to put an end to the life of another.

Cynthia Darwin, for all he knew, might have been an odious woman, might even have been involved in the death of her first husband: her character was irrelevant. Someone, someone perhaps known to Carolus, had gone to her cabin and having been trustingly admitted, had strangled the wretched woman. And although Carolus had boasted that he had certain theories or ideas about the identity of the murderer, he had to admit that they were too vague and remote to be formulated, even to himself.

85

Sitting in the lounge, he could scrutinize the very people who might be suspected because they at least had the opportunity, and although many of them seemed hopelessly improbable by reason of their characters as far as Carolus knew them, he was too experienced to dismiss them from a list of the potentially guilty. Susan Berry for example. Could one imagine that rabbit-mouthed and frustrated nymphomaniac strangling another woman and quite a sturdy-looking one at that? She was compounded of jealousies and longings, but how could she feel jealous of Cynthia Darwin except perhaps for the money which enabled the woman to dress well? Susan Berry had not even seen Guy Darwin—so far as was known—at the time when Cynthia was murdered. Carolus was ready to admit that envy and frustration could carry women to extraordinary lengths, but Susan, like everyone else on board, escaped anything like real suspicion.

Like Patty Spittals, for instance. A silly, kindly woman devoted to the husband she pretended to deride, and amused by his wealth rather than purse-proud or seriously pretentious. It was true that she had every opportunity and might easily have built up enough confidence between herself and the dead woman to be admitted to her cabin at once, as the murderer had been. But what possible motive could she have had? She had been on the cruise last year when Cynthia's first husband had died and been buried at sea and nothing was yet known to Carolus of her behaviour at that time towards the widow, but Patty was a good-natured woman and it was difficult to imagine her in the more sinister role.

The same applied to her husband. It was stretching the imagination too far altogether to imagine the ex-Mayor and millionaire with the solemn manner, which he often broke by a wink, feeling such animosity towards Cynthia Darwin that he would go to her cabin and strangle her, but there was, of course, the

precedent of Macbeth and his wife and the power of Patty
Spittals over her husband might account for some of that animosity. He, too, had the opportunity and the fact that his wife
so firmly denied having heard anything at all from the next
cabin, while Susan Berry supposed she had heard the murderer's
knock, kept Sir Charles in the circle of possibilities.

Nor could Porteous be dismissed out of hand. He was a
man with an obsession, and such men are dangerous. He had
spent his life building up the business of Summertime Cruises
and would obviously do anything to preserve it, as he had
shown in his callous behaviour on two occasions already. What
connection this could have with the murder of one of his passengers Carolus was at a loss to imagine, but he was convinced that if the existence of Cynthia Darwin threatened
Porteous's schemes, he would not scruple to rid himself of her
in even the most violent way. Whether Ratchett would follow
him, or even keep silence for his sake was extremely doubtful:
Carolus had seen how deluded Porteous was when he spoke
of the loyalty of such men as Ratchett. But Porteous was the
"boss" and among men of Ratchett's type that counted for a
lot, whether he wished it to or no.

When Carolus came to consider Captain Scorer as a po-
tential murderer, he decided that he was beyond all probabilities. First, he could see no conceivable motive; second, the
opportunity, though not entirely impossible, was far-fetched;
and third, Scorer was certainly not a man who could ever be
suspected by a sane observer of any such action. Carolus hesitated to erase him from his imaginary list only because the
Captain was, after all, on board his ship, and had, as Carolus
had gathered from the Purser, not invited Cynthia Darwin to
sit at his table. It would be ingenious to imagine a murder
being committed for the sake of a place at the Captain's table,
and to Carolus, who had known equally strange motives, it

was not impossible, but to suppose that the Captain himself
might act against a woman who had once sat near him in the
dining hall was idiotic. Yet there was something about Scorer
that made Carolus keep him in mind.

As he certainly kept Alexander Carlisle. He liked the West
Indian and felt a certain respect for a man so obviously self-
dependent, so much a master of his own fate, but he found it
quite easy to picture him silently opening Cynthia's cabin door
and entering. Nor did Carolus think it impossible that Cynthia
had invited him to do so. The snag here, as with so many of
the passengers, was lack of any recognizable motive, but since
Carolus still had more than a week among them, he believed
that a motive would eventually appear.

A more promising possibility, if only because Carolus knew
so little about him, was the man who had announced himself
to the Purser as Dr Runwell. Those sharp grey eyes, that keen
unfriendly look, might mean anything. Carolus realized that
he had not seen Dr Runwell since that first encounter on deck.
Perhaps he sat behind Carolus in the dining hall, but surely
sometimes he must come out on deck? There was nothing to
point at him, nothing whatever, yet Carolus lingered for some
time over him, and, as if by some curious speak-of-the-Devil
kind of superstition, he suddenly noticed the man himself sitting quite alone on the other side of the saloon. He was not
reading or apparently taking any interest in his fellow passengers. He just sat bolt upright and looked ahead. "I'm taking
this cruise purely for my health," Carolus remembered him
saying. Well, perhaps.

Then there was Medlow, too obviously a "suspect" to be
suspected at all. His deliberately crazy manner and loud voice,
his noisy disapproval of everyone and everything about him
and his claim to be making a report of some kind as though he
were a member of MI5—all suggested that he was almost ask-

ing to be suspected, and unless this were a sinister double bluff, Medlow could be dismissed from Carolus's mind.

Not so "the lady at the table where we sit." Mrs Grahame-Willows might well be that gossiping mischief-maker familiar to all who spend long periods on ship, but there might be other motives for the stories she set circulating. There seemed to be too much design in her exaggerations, too much sheer fantasy in her stories, to be completely ingenuous and the rapidity with which she always produced her explanations after each event was in itself suspicious. That Carolus had accepted her as a figure of comedy when described by Mrs Stick was not in itself a complete contradiction.

But Carolus moved on to Dr Yaqub Ali. Had these been the days of Sherlock Holmes, any Asian would have been per se a suspect and Carolus felt bound to remember the circumstances of Tom Travers's death, but he did not seriously suppose that the doctor had murdered Cynthia Darwin or had any part in her murder. He could, he admitted, be wrong and at this stage, when so few of his ideas led to any reasonable conclusion, he could not afford utterly to wipe out Dr Yaqub Ali's name.

There remained the young man Gavin Ritchie who used makeup and the blonde girl who so very pointedly had not come aboard with him or been seen with him since then. But Ritchie's passionate friendship with the Assistant Purser, though it did not clear him entirely, was a circumstance that made his involvement in a violent act somewhat improbable. Of the Assistant Purser, it was possible to imagine brutality, but there had been nothing to suggest that he, or Susan Berry's friend the Second Engineer, had any sort of involvement other than the fact, true of all the officers and crew, that they served on a ship on which a man was believed to have been lost overboard and on which a woman passenger had been killed. Or perhaps the fact—again learned from the Purser—that they had all been serving on the same ship a year ago when the woman's rich husband died and was buried at sea, was enough to make them be considered as suspects.

There was another couple named Popple, and yet another whose name Carolus had not even troubled to ascertain; three single men who played gin rummy all day, and a couple of nondescript girls with whom he had not spoken. There were also the members of the cheerful Irish family.

This left, of all those known to him who had been on board at the time of Cynthia Darwin's murder, no one but the deckhand Leacock, and with him Carolus admitted there was something of a problem. Leacock drank, and yet was emphatically considered by Porteous an "excellent fellow." He was quarrelsome, as Carolus observed, yet seemed to be put in a position of trust by the ship's officers. He was moreover indiscreet and talkative, the last man, one would have thought, allowed to be on familiar terms with the passengers. There was in fact some mystery about him. Carolus did not go so far as to suspect him of murder, but he felt that although Leacock had been ready, perhaps too ready, to answer all his questions, he could have told Carolus very much more, and nearer the point, than he had done.

"I hope," said a voice beside Carolus, "that you do not exclude me from your suspects of the crime, which I see you all too obviously trying to elucidate?" It was Mr Gorringer and he took the seat beside Carolus. "Although our long relationship might be expected to protect me, yet a good detective must surely have no friends. I am willing, no, I positively insist on being considered among the possibilities."

"Very well," said Carolus curtly. "Where were you at the time of Mrs Darwin's murder, that is to say between one and two in the small hours?"

Mr Gorringer was equally curt, even somewhat snappish.
"In my bunk," he said.

"To which you naturally have no witnesses?"

"Certainly not."

"Then you are on my list, in so far as I have one, along
with the rest of the passengers and crew of this ship."

"Are you not, perhaps, carrying a joke too far, my, dear
Deene? My suggestion was a facetious one and should have
been seen by you as such. I should be distressed if you did not
credit me with as ready a sense of humour as your own. But
be that as it may, we shall, I think, congratulate ourselves tomorrow when the body of our fellow passenger has been removed from the ship and placed on board a homebound
aeroplane. Then and then only shall I feel that a true holiday
will begin for all of us."

"You will? I shall feel on the contrary, that I must get down
to some really hard work."

"Will you not, if I may use a somewhat inappropriate meta-
phor, be seeking to shut the stable door when the horse has gone?"

Carolus looked serious.

"I hope not," he said. "I truly hope not. Unless of course
you are referring to the late Mrs Darwin as a horse."

"Certainly not. I warned you that I was speaking in meta-
phor. You are too ready to misunderstand me."

There was a long silence between them. Then Mr Gorringer remarked reflectively, "So we shall approach Calpe, one
of the Pillars of Hercules of the ancients, tomorrow."

"You mean we reach Gibraltar," said Carolus.

"I do. It will be a sad approach to those of us who es-
teemed the poor lady whose remains will be taken ashore by
her husband."

"But that mustn't prevent your seeing the famous apes,"
said Carolus. "They so exactly resemble the Lower Fifth at

Newminster. And now, before turning in, I must consult Mrs Stick. She keeps me informed of the more sensational rumours. Goodnight, headmaster."

He found Mrs Stick on deck with her husband.

"Thank goodness you've come, sir. I don't think I could have gone on much longer," she said, leaving Stick and joining Carolus. "Stick was set on going round the deck twenty-four times and I was feeling half blown away by the wind, though it's not so bad as last night. If we was to go into the Sun Lounge for a minute I've got something I think you ought to hear about."

Carolus willingly followed the little woman in.

"She says," Mrs Stick began at once, "that the Port Authorities in Gibraltar won't hear of it, sending a lady ashore in a coffin when nobody can say how she came to die. I mean, it does sound a bit on the off side, doesn't it? So I suppose we shall know all the rest of the cruise that she's lying in her cabin dead, as you might say."

"I might, but I promise you I won't. Your friend is quite incorrect. The whole thing has been arranged by wireless. The body will be taken ashore before the passengers are out of their cabins in the early morning."

"There! I told Her She must be mistaken, but you know what She is once she gets an idea in Her head. Wild elephants won't move it. But She did happen to say that She thinks a Dr Runwell had something to do with it—the murder, I mean. She says She doesn't like the look of this Dr Runwell at all. She says he might easily have stuck a knife in anyone."

"But Mrs Darwin died of strangulation."

"So they say. But how does anyone know? All we know is the poor lady went to bed and never got up next morning. That's all we've been told. She says she might have been poisoned or had her throat cut for all we can tell. Nor She doesn't much like the look of that doctor, anyway. She says all She knows is, She wouldn't like to have anything wrong with her when he's around, that's all, She says. She says he'd operate on you as soon as look at you, She says."

Then Mrs Stick added a few observations of her own which roused a keener interest in Carolus.

"You know that young plump party with the blonde hair, don't you?" The description was adequate and Carolus nodded. "Well, I may be mistaken but you can't help noticing things, can you?"

Carolus waited.

"It's the man whose wife's been done for," said Mrs Stick, and once again was silent.

"What about him? Or her?" Carolus asked obligingly.

"They were together all yesterday evening, that's what. Sitting together as though they couldn't take their eyes off each other. Mind you, she is an attractive girl, whatever anyone says. But it's a bit quick, isn't it, when his poor wife's only just been murdered. I mentioned it to Her, but She doesn't think there's anything in it. She says people only come on a cruise like this to have a good time. So I said, 'Not when their wife's been murdered, or shouldn't do,' I said. She's very funny in that way. If anyone else notices something She won't have it."

Carolus seemed to be considering Mrs Stick's observations. "You're quite sure?" he asked.

"Sure as I'm sitting here. That Mr Darwin, it was, and the young party they call Rita, though Rita What I don't know. They were sitting side by side looking at each other. Whatever happened afterwards I don't know."

"Afterwards?"

"When we all went to bed, I mean. But by the way they were looking at each other—well! You'd never have thought he'd come on the ship to find his wife done away with. Not that he doesn't seem quite a nice fellow when he talks to you. It may all be on that Rita's side. But what I say is, it didn't look like it."

Carolus felt that a comment was being demanded of him and did his best. "You never know," he said. It was enough.

"Of course you don't," said Mrs Stick. "Not when it's one of those blonde girls like that. Perhaps she's after his money."

"How would she know he has any?"

"She told me that. He's got ever such a big business, She said. Something to do with television, She said, so he's bound to make a lot. This Rita only had just enough to book her passage, She says. So there you are."

And there in fact Carolus was and there was Mrs Stick when the two of them decided to go to bed and, as Mrs Stick said, "wait and see in the morning."

Ten

BY BREAKFAST TIME IT was all over—the coffin had gone ashore followed by Guy Darwin and before midday Mr Porteous, who had accompanied the bereaved husband, reported to Carolus that he had seen them both, Darwin and the coffin, on a plane taking off for London.

"So I hope we shan't hear any more of that," said Porteous.

Carolus did not share the aspiration.

"You don't seriously think that you can get rid of the situation as simply as this, do you? The thing is only beginning, and you must surely be aware of it. Just because Darwin has shown himself understanding of your problems, you needn't think they don't exist."

"What problems? I think you take a very gloomy view of it all, Deene. Holiday cruises have been interrupted by unfortunate circumstances of this kind before now, you know, and the company organizing them has survived."

"If you mean by 'unfortunate circumstances of this kind' the murder of a woman passenger in her cabin, I doubt it. There was a famous case once, I remember, when a steward murdered a young woman who had acted in films. But that was on a transatlantic crossing, not on a holiday cruise. And certainly not when the husband of the same woman had died on the same ship just a year earlier."

"That was unfortunate, as I told you at our first meeting, but there is no evidence, that I know of, to connect it with this."

"No? You have the wonderful faculty of deliberate blindness," said Carolus. "Sometimes I envy you. But not now. It's through your blindness in this case that you are walking into danger."

"Danger? What kind of danger?" asked Mr Porteous, with more concern than he had hitherto shown.

"Just danger," said Carolus airily, and left the impresario of holiday pleasures to think it over.

After lunch, Carolus ignored Mrs Stick waving with some agitation from the door of the Sun Lounge and went in search of Dr Yaqub Ali. Perhaps something Mr Porteous had said had suggested a line of thought to him or perhaps he had intended, when a suitable moment arrived, to interview the Pakistani ship's surgeon.

Dr Yaqub Ali was a youngish rather handsome man who looked well in uniform and seemed to know it.

"I have wanted for some time to have a chat with you," Carolus began. "You know that I'm trying to get at the truth about this murder."

Dr Ali spoke in a clipped voice and did not sound too friendly.

"I understood that you had been employed to prevent a murder, not to solve the mystery of one," he said.

"Both," said Carolus. "And both murders, for that matter."

"I don't follow you."

"The murder of Mrs Darwin and that of her first husband a year ago."

"Really? You doubtless know more about the circumstances of the death of Mr Travers than I do. I only examined the body and signed a death certificate," said the doctor sarcastically.

"Yes. That's about all. And you were too seasick to do either of them conscientiously. So let's get down to realities. What do you really think Travers died of?"

"Coronary thrombosis, as I wrote in the certificate I gave him. And I'd like to see you prove it was anything else."

"Prove, no. Suspect, yes. But you may not have realized it fully when you wrote the certificate. Seasickness can be a terrible thing."

"So can a suspicious detective. Perhaps you are going to tell me what killed Mrs Darwin?"

"Yes. Strangulation. Very quickly and violently carried out as it had to be, to be unheard. An entirely different case. Travers was probably poisoned."

"You know everything, Mr Deene. Perhaps you also know who administered the poison?"

"Yes. I think I know that too. But I admit to being unsure in that case. I was hoping you would help me. Who do *you* think it was?"

Dr Ali smiled, but not amiably.

"Really. You have a nerve. You come to tell me that I gave a dishonest or at least a mistaken death certificate, a very serious matter to a man in my position, though a trivial one it would seem in the eyes of a private detective, and you then ask me to assist you in your wrong-headed investigations."

"That's it," said Carolus blithely.

"Then," said Dr Yaqub Ali, losing his temper, "do you know what I say? I say, go to hell."

"Quite. That would be most convenient for you. In the meantime I must remind you that you have entered into a dangerous conspiracy with Porteous and others and will certainly have to answer for it when we reach London. Mrs Darwin must have some relations apart from her recently acquired husband."

"You put that very crudely. I was present at the wedding, and can assure you . . ."

"Oh, yes. It was a love-match on one side anyway. I don't dispute that. I only said 'recently acquired' because you, and perhaps only you, doctor, know the exact circumstances of her widowhood."

"Let us stop beating about the shrub," said Dr Ali, voicing his first Orientalism. "You think Mrs Darwin was murdered, don't you? Perhaps you suspect me of the murder?"

"I always suspect unnecessary secrecy in such a matter."

"Yes. I thought so."

"What I would like to know is what took you to Mrs Darwin's cabin? How did you discover that she was dead?"

"There, I fear, you touch on the Hippocratic oath. It was a fellow doctor who called me."

"You mean Dr Runwell?"

"Since he is the only other doctor on board, you must be correct. But I prefer that the matter should not be made public. Dr Runwell, I gather, had known Mrs Darwin before her second marriage . . ."

"But during her first?"

"Possibly, yes. I have no information except what he told me, that he and Mrs Travers, as he called her, had been friends for some years. Whether or not they were lovers is not for me to say."

"If they were, the woman must have had charms which were not obvious to others. Go on."

"It seems, not to put too sharp an edge on it, that they had arranged that Runwell call at Cynthia Darwin's cabin during the night, for what he described as a chat. I did not ask him to go into any further detail. It was not my business."

"But it damned well will be, when a coroner gets his teeth into you. Or haven't you thought of that? Your Hippocratic oath will go out the window and you'll have to speak the truth. What did he find?"

"Just what I found not long after. The woman was in her bunk. She had been strangled before she could call for help."

"By someone whose knock she had mistaken for Runwell? Or by Runwell himself?"

"I think you can dismiss that from possibility."

"Why?"

"Because he would scarcely have called me if he had strangled Mrs Darwin, would he?"

"It's hard to say. At all events, that's how you came to find the body?"

"Exactly. Are you satisfied now? Or do you still think I killed her?"

"I have never accused you. I'm glad you've cleared up one thing that mystified me. It may well be that you're unable to clear up more."

"Just as, in your particular line, Mr Deene, you're unable to account for things that to a simple medico like me would seem to demand explanation."

"Such as?"

"Such as the cry of 'Man Overboard' on our first night out. That, so far as I know, has never been satisfactorily explained."

"No. It hasn't. Can you explain it?"

"I know the deckhand Leacock to be a drunkard."

"Yes? Then why is he put in a position of trust?"

"Ask me a new one," said the doctor, confusing his colloquialisms.

"It's an interesting point," said Carolus. "Do you think he knows something which Porteous does not want known?"

"Could be. He's a bit of a sly shoes, I think, But it seems certain that if anyone went overboard it was a stowaway. Everyone else was accounted for. Leacock may have seen something and certainly there were the clothes. I should have thought your job was to question Leacock instead of wasting your time on my humble self, as you say."

"I haven't wasted my time, doctor, and you are not humble. But you have given me an idea. Thank you and good-night."

Mrs Stick was still waiting near the door of the Sun Lounge. She showed signs of impatience, but by a wave of her hand told Carolus that she was still anxious to tell him something.

"Wait till I tell you what's happened," she said excitedly, and Carolus, who seemed to have no option in the matter, waited obediently.

"It's a sailor this time," she said, then in her infuriating way, having thrown her grenade, waited for results.

"Not dead?" asked Carolus.

"He might as well be for all the good it will do him. It's that sailor who's always round the decks with a vulgar name, if you take it that way."

"Leacock?" suggested Carolus.

"That's him. What do you think he was on to Stick about?"

Carolus knew when in his turn to remain silent.

"First it was harmless enough, about the man who went overboard on the first night and how he'd stared at this sailor with his eyes all fiery and looked as though he was going to stick a knife in him."

"That's quite new," commented Carolus.

"So it may be but it isn't the terrible part."

"Don't say he pushed the man over the side?"

"He may well have done but he didn't tell Stick that. He began to get on to this place we're going to next."

"Tunis. What about it?"

"Everything about it if you ask me. He told Stick he always goes ashore there. It seems they're only allowed ashore in one of the places we stop at and quite enough too, when you hear what I have to tell you. It seems he always chooses this next place where the dates come from. Not that he has much time for buying dates when he gets off of the ship and in one way I don't blame him, I've always said they were nasty sticky things. They say the Arabians can live on a few of these dates for days if they get lost in the desert. Well, let them, is what I say. I shouldn't care for it myself. But what I was going to say was what this sailor told Stick he always did when he got ashore in this place."

"Yes?" prompted Carolus.

"I don't hardly like to tell you, sir, even though we are aboard a ship where there is liable to be a murder at any moment. This sailor with the vulgar name told Stick he goes to a place called Madame Fifi's and you can guess what that is. And the worst part of it is he asked Stick to go with him. Can you imagine it?"

Carolus was bound to admit he could not.

"Just think of it, every time this ship comes into this place, where they say the Arabians step on the boxes of dates with their bare feet, if you can take my meaning, sir, this sailor goes to this Madame Fifi's. You can guess what goes on there."

"I can, yes," admitted Carolus.

"And what's more tries to get Stick to go with him."

"What did Stick say to that?"

"Stick comes from a respectable home and when it comes to anything like that he'd no more dream of going with this sailor than flying to the moon. He told him straight. 'You can go after these fancy women,' he said, 'but leave me out of it,' he said. 'I'd rather have a pint of beer,' Stick said. And d'you know what this sailor said to that? 'You can't get it,' he said, 'so you might as well have the other.' That's what he said. I was right down disgusted when Stick told me."

"No wonder," said Carolus.

"But that wasn't the end of it. He still tried to get Stick to go with him. 'We dock in the morning,' he says, 'so you'll have all day to do anything you want. I shall wait for you at Madame Fifi's at about nine o'clock in the evening,' he said, 'because we have to be on board by eleven o'clock and sail at midnight and the town's some way from the docks,' he said. Stick said he had quite a job to tell him he wasn't coming and the sailor with the vulgar name was ever so disappointed. Can you beat that?"

Carolus could not, so he bade Mrs Stick goodnight. As he did so the little woman's face lit up.

"There She is!" she exclaimed. "Just come in now. The lady at the table where we sit. I'll bring Her over and you can see whether She tells the truth or no."

Carolus agreed, and soon Mrs Grahame-Willows joined them. She was a somewhat gaunt lady with frilly clothes and a quantity of inexpensive jewellery.

"I've heard such a lot about you," she told Carolus in a carefully refined voice.

Carolus would liked to have told her that it was nothing to the quantity he had heard about her, but desisted.

"It seems you're quite a detective," went on Mrs Grahame-Willows. "Have you managed to clear up our mysteries on board this ship?"

"Pretty well, I think," said Carolus.

Mrs Stick was anxious to show off her friend at her best.

"Tell him about the Assistant Purser," she suggested.

"Oh, that's nothing," said Mrs Grahame-Willows modestly. "It just seems that he's being turned off the ship after this voyage. Anyone could see that would happen as soon as we came on board, but I never thought it would come to murder with Mrs Darwin, did you?"

"*What* would come to murder?" asked Carolus.

"You must have seen," Mrs Grahame-Willows told him. "I mean you couldn't help it, surely. That Dr Runwell and her. I don't know how you didn't spot it at once."

"Perhaps it takes a trained eye," suggested Carolus.

"Of course when it came to the schoolmaster who played Scrabble with her I could tell there was nothing in it. A little footy-footy under the table, that was all. But Dr Runwell. . . . Of course, they'd known each other before. It was all arranged before they came on board. They only had to pass a note to each other at the bar, saying he'd come to her cabin at such a time, and there was nothing more to it."

"I see," nodded Carolus. "It must have been a great shock to him to find her dead?"

"Of course it was. It was touch and go whether he would throw himself into the water or not."

"I wonder how you know that," said Carolus.

"This lady knows everything," said Mrs Stick loyally. "There's nothing goes on She doesn't know about."

"Very interesting," said Carolus, who was growing a trifle tired of the lady at the table where we sit and wanted to go to bed.

"I tell Her She can see into the future. She could make a fortune at it when we get back to England, I tell Her," said Mrs Stick. "That's if we ever get back," she added rather mournfully.

"We may not *all* get back," said Mrs Grahame-Willows. "But I see no danger for most of us."

"That's good," said Carolus briskly. "And goodnight."

Eleven

CAROLUS TOOK A MINI-TAXI from the docks into Tunis. Driving for several miles across the marshy wasteland and shallow waters that divide the city from the seaside groups of villas, with names that recalled old battles and human sacrifices, he felt there was something sinister about the whole region, something that recalled Salammbo and the cruel and vicious history of Carthage. The flocks of flamingos glimpsed across the cheerless wasteland only emphasized the impression, and when he came into the pretentious boulevard of Tunis itself and saw the severe-looking Berber countenances, he wanted to return to the ship. But he had some work to do. If his theory was correct, it was here that he would discover the whole ugly truth.

He told the taxi driver, a bearded man with a hostile squint, to drop him off at the Café de Paris which he knew to be the principal meeting place of the town, and entering it he realized that a British naval ship was in port for *matelots* were scattered about the large room.

He found an empty table but was soon joined by a couple of his fellow-countrymen.

"Have you been here before?" asked Carolus.

They both said they had.

"Do you know a brothel called Madame Fifi's?"

After a break for loud guffaws, they told him that everyone knew it, the lousiest dump in the town, adding that if he
wanted a whore-shop with a bit more class they could direct
him to one. They looked astounded when Carolus explained
that he had business at Madame Fifi's and that, much though
he would like to have accepted their invitation, he had to refuse.

"You kinky or something?" one of them asked. "There's
none of them there under fifty. They're not fit for human con-
sumption, I can promise you."

Carolus had to make some kind of explanation while they
looked at him with blank incredulity.

"Hope you have a good time then," they said as they left,
obviously not meaning it.

Carolus remained sitting at his table, watching the glass
doors which opened on to the pavements of the Avenue
Bourguiba, and soon realized that he was not alone in knowing that this café was a general meeting place which even his
fellow passengers could not miss.

The first to arrive was Susan Berry in a light summer frock
and, to the surprise of Carolus, quite alone. Where, he wondered, was the Second Engineer? Surely Miss Berry had not
again been left to come ashore alone? No, evidently not, for
she was followed into the café by a sleek and dressy Tunisian
with frizzy hair and a self-consciously smug manner.

Carolus changed his place at his table to become invisible
to the girl, but not quite out of earshot, for bits of conversation between the two came across to him undrowned by the
noise of coffee cups and conversation.

"Mohammed!" he heard Susan say, and again more feel-
ingly, "Oh, Mohammed!"

The gigolo did most of the talking, but in a low voice, and
Carolus could only catch the name that Miss Berry had adopted
or which Mohammed had given her. "Suzanne. You are so

preety, Suzanne!" he began to whisper and it was several minutes before Carolus heard him say, "In my motor car . . . Only
you and me . . . You are so preety!"

When Lady Spittals came in alone, Susan was unwise
enough to use her name and title to Mohammed, who seemed
to be mesmerized.

"Lady Spittals! Does that not mean the wife of a Lord?" he
asked Susan quite loudly so that Carolus heard him distinctly.

"No," said Susan sharply. "She's no one. Oh, come along,
Mohammed. You're going to take me for a car ride. Never
mind her!"

Rather regretfully, Carolus thought, the Tunisian rose and
ushered Miss Berry from the café. He might have looked even
more regretful had not Sir Charles come in to join his wife.

When Susan and her new friend had gone, Carolus moved
to a place at the Spittals' table.

"What a town!" said Patty Spittals. "We can't get over it!
I want to go to the Medina where all the souvenir shops are
but he won't budge, of course. He says they're full of rubbish.
I don't know how he can tell if he hasn't been. Did you see
poor Susan? Got off with a guide, it looks like. We've seen
several more from the ship, too. I was surprised to see Mr
Ratchett in the Avenoo. You'd have thought he'd be busy on
board ship at a time like this. And who do you think took Mrs
Grahame-Willows ashore this morning? The doctor! I'd like
to know where they were going, wouldn't you?"

"No," said Carolus, but with a smile and, asking Sir
Charles what he would drink, called the waiter.

"Of course I expected to see the West Indian ashore," went
on Patty Spittals.

"Why?" Carolus asked.

"Oh, I mean . . . well, he'll feel quite at home here, I should
think. He has very nice manners, hasn't he?"

"Why not?"

"Oh, I don't know. You can't tell what to expect nowadays. I'm glad I persuaded Charles to come this time. I call it interesting. You wouldn't really think you were so near Europe, would you. It's more like what you read about in the *Arabian Nights*. Mind you, I shouldn't care to live here. Give me good old Surrey, any day. But this is what we've come for, isn't it? To see strange places, I mean. One young darkie wanted Charles to go with him to a Turkish Bath—I can't think why unless he was a pickpocket. Charles said 'Another time!' He always says 'another time' when anyone asks him to do anything. Well, we must be getting along. There's that young couple just come in. I'm glad they've got to know each other at last."

"Which young couple?"

"The good-looking young man and the blonde. Gavin Ritchie I think he's called. Come along, Charles."

"Where are we going?" asked the ex-Mayor.

"We'll take a taxi. It's not far to where all the shops are and they sell all sorts of things there. Leather work and all sorts."

She managed to drag her husband out into the street, and through the windows Carolus saw her waving to a taxi.

At nearly nine o'clock Carolus went out of the café and called a taxi. This one was so small that he had to sit hunched at the back with his head almost between his knees.

The taxi driver was in no way surprised when Carolus told him to go to Madame Fifi's, but said in French that he couldn't drive right there, the street was closed to traffic, but he would leave him nearby.

Sitting in his cramped position, like a question mark, Carolus could not see which of the ways they took but was relieved at last when the midget taxi came to a halt and he could unwind himself and stand up.

He was in a narrow street with very little lighting. The taxi driver, after naming a generous fare, told Carolus that if he walked straight on he would find a lighted doorway to his right. That would be Madame Fifi's. Carolus saw dark figures moving in the direction pointed out by the taxi driver, but near him there was no one at all. He paid for his taxi and in a moment found himself alone.

From his knowledge of North Africa, Carolus did not feel actual fear in that dark and reeking side street between windowless houses, but when he was addressed from the darkness quite near at hand, he started.

"Want Madame Fifi's?" a deep voice enquired in the authentic English of the London suburbs.

Carolus admitted it.

"Shouldn't go there if I was you," said the voice, and when the man became visible for a moment in the lights of a reversing car, Carolus perceived that he was a stringy-looking individual with a moulting moustache.

"So I have been told once this evening by two naval advocates for a different brothel, doubtless called Madame Mimi's."

"No, it's not. It's called Madame Lucille's and it's much better than this. See, what happens here is that if the police find girls who are trying to work on their own, they run them in at once. They won't have freelancing in this town. They keep them in quad for a month or two, then they take them to one of the cathouses run officially and supervised by the police. 'In you go' they say, and that's the last the girl sees the light of day. They say that whores have to work for the state, not pocket their earnings for themselves. Reasonable, isn't it?"

"No. What about this one? Madame Fifi's?"

"Just the same. Official, see? The Madame's a sort of manageress. It's her job not to let any of the girls get away."

"So Madame Fifi is not her name?"

"Good lord, no. I've known three different Madame Fifis since I've been in Tunis and that's only about five years. But I shouldn't go in tonight, if I were you."

"Why?"

"There was a bit of trouble when I called in a while ago. The police will be round any minute."

"But you say it's quite legitimate?"

"So it is, but the police aren't so particular about anyone they find here when there's been a fight. I should go to Madame Lucille's if I were you. I'll show you the way."

Carolus had suspected all along that the beachcombing Englishman would make this proposition.

"Sorry," he said, "I've got business here," and passing the man some Tunisian paper money, the value of which he would not have known even if he could see it, he walked on.

From the lighted doorway to his right a bulky woman waddled out.

"You a sailor?" she asked in bad but comprehensible French. Carolus thought it best to say yes.

"Come in then, please. There has been some trouble here with some of yours. Fighting one another. You see."

Carolus did not want to see, unless he would thus find Leacock. He realized it was probably no good making enquiries for him. He would be in civilian clothes. And how was Madame Fifi, the present holder of the title, to know him? But he tried.

"Was a man here who comes regularly?" he asked. "Once every six weeks or so? A strong man. Drinks a lot. Likes fighting."

"That's him. That's the man who made trouble this evening. He's a *marin de commerce,* what you call a merchant seaman. He came in here and chose a girl, the same one he always has. They go upstairs, when in comes another man, looking for him. He was fairly drunk, but so was the other who had gone upstairs. So I say nothing. I don't want trouble here. But this second man he climbs the stairs and starts shouting the name. Li-Co, it sounded like. 'Li-Co!' he shouts and the first man comes out and they start fighting. It is terrible. First one falls down, then the other and at last this Li-Co falls down insensible. So the other drags him towards the room where he was with the girl—she has run downstairs—and it sounds as though he drags him inside, and maybe looks in his pockets. I don't know. I know I never looked in any pockets. Then the second man runs downstairs and out into the street. He is gone. Quick. He'll never come back.

"So Li-Co is on the floor upstairs and none of the girls dare to go near him. I daren't go either so as you are a friend of his will you go?"

"Who said I was a friend of his?"

"You say you are a sailor. That's what Li-Co is. Also the other man. I can tell them. You take him away in a taxi so he keeps out of trouble. Everything is known round here and someone will tell the police and they come and shut me up. And take Li-Co too."

"Too bad," said Carolus, "All right, I'll have a look at Li-Co."

"Then you take him with you to the ship, that's right?"

"Let me see him," said Carolus and Madame Fifi led the way through the lighted door, closing it firmly behind her. A small man, pockmarked and diseased-looking, took over as guardian.

"He doesn't let the girls pass," commented Madame Fifi. "They're very much afraid of him. Come upstairs."

Again she led the way, but at the top of the stairs she turned.

"That's it. Number Four. Over there. That's where you'll find Li-Co."

She seemed impatient to go downstairs again and left Carolus standing there. After a moment he knocked at the door of
number four, and when there was no reply from within
knocked louder. When he had knocked once more he tried the
handle and found that the door was locked.

He stood back and kicked at the lower panel.

"Not so loud!" called Madame Fifi. "It will bring the police!"

"That's just what we need," said Carolus. "Go and call
them! Are you sure he's in here?"

"Yes. Yes. He's there!"

Carolus kicked at the lock itself and at last the door fell
open.

The room stank. Cheap perfume, perspiration and another
acrid smell. On the floor was Leacock with a bloody wound
in his shoulder. He was dead.

Why the shoulder? Carolus wondered stupidly. Then there
came back to him from a school classroom the words of Old
Buzzy who used to teach him classics.

"Between the shoulder blades," he had said of a Greek or
Roman statue (Carolus couldn't remember which) illustrated
in his textbook of a young man committing suicide by driving
a sword downward from the left shoulder.

"Quickest way to the heart," said Old Buzzy and not until
this moment did Carolus realize that it was true.

He kept his head. He went slowly to the door and began
descending the stairs. He guessed that Madame Fifi knew what
he had seen, but he had no intention of admitting it and so
becoming involved in a highly unpleasant situation.

"He's all right," he said. "Sleeping it off. Don't disturb
him for a while. I will come back later for him with a taxi and
bring some friends to carry him if he can't walk. You say the
man he fought was also a sailor?"

"I think so. He wore no uniform. But since he was that man's friend . . ."

"Yes, yes. He too has probably gone to get a taxi. We will take him on the ship very soon. You keep quiet, continue with your ordinary business and all will be well."

Then Carolus walked out into the narrow street and made for the slightly wider one where his taxi had left him. By the luckiest of chances one of the minicabs—the only ones to be found in Tunis, he realized—approached him. He screwed himself into it and managed to tell the driver that he should go straight out to La Goulette where his ship lay.

When he came aboard the *Summer Queen* he was grudgingly greeted by a deckhand he had once seen talking with Leacock.

"You haven't seen anything of my mate while you were ashore, have you?" this one asked and Carolus, pretending to be preoccupied, managed not to answer. He made for the Bridge and was relieved to find both Captain Scorer and Mr Porteous.

"I'm afraid you've lost your best deckhand," he said bluntly.

"What do mean by 'lost'? Leacock has gone ashore, with permission."

"He won't return," said Carolus, "and I advise you to sail as soon as possible."

"What is all this?" asked the Captain impatiently.

"I'm telling you about Leacock. He's been murdered."

Porteous excelled himself in asking inane questions.

"Where?" he gasped.

"Shortest way down to the heart."

"What's the matter with you, Deene? I meant where was he when he . . . met with an accident?"

"In a brothel. And it was no accident," said Carolus sharply.

"You mean to say that Leacock has been murdered?" said Porteous.

"That's what I said."

Porteous's next was of course "How?"

"Longish knife. Into the heart. By this time his blood will be seeping through into the room below. If you don't get the ship out of this port within about half an hour I doubt if you'll be allowed to sail at all. Your cruisers will contemplate mudflats for the next week or so while you're attending enquiries."

"We're due to sail at midnight," said Porteous. "We can't go before that. Some of the passengers may be still ashore."

"You do what you like, but I'd advise you to get the hell out of here before they find Leacock."

Porteous became the man of action.

"Have a check made, Captain Scorer. See who's still ashore and whether any of the crew are. We'll sail as soon as we can."

"I devoutly hope that's soon enough."

"In a *brothel*," said Porteous, and then, as Carolus anticipated, "What was he doing in a brothel?"

"I leave you to guess," said Carolus sweetly.

"No, don't go, Deene," pleaded Porteous. "Have you any idea how the poor fellow came to meet his death?"

"Yes. Like Christopher Marlowe. In a drunken brawl."

"With another sailor? In that case we must take every step to bring the man to justice."

"How do you know it was a man?"

"Fairly obvious, isn't it?" said Porteous, regaining some of his old superior manner. "You would scarcely expect to find a woman in a brothel, would you?"

"I should scarcely expect to find anyone else," Carolus replied gravely. "But I see what you mean. Leacock was murdered, they tell me, in a place known as Madame Fifi's, by a fellow sailor, but neither of them was in uniform. They quar-relled, believe it or not, over a girl, a middle-aged whore to be exact, who was apparently Leacock's choice whenever the ship came into Tunis."

"Great heavens!"

"That is when he wasn't too drunk to see one from an-other," went on Carolus.

"I thought he was our best man," groaned Porteous.

"He may have been a good seaman," admitted Carolus. Then he turned and said seriously to Porteous, "Look here. I think I can clear up this whole mess as soon as we reach Lon-don. But only on one condition. If it becomes known to any-one aboard, to *anyone* mark you, I can do nothing at all. I mean this. This ship, like Shakespeare's isle, is full of noises and there are ears attuned to the least rumour from them. Let it be known to one single person that you are aware of what has happened to Leacock and you're a ruined man. He has been left adrift here. That's all."

"Why are you so emphatic?"

"Because I want to prove my theory's right and I shall never do so if the slightest murmur of what I have told you gets about. I will do what I can to check gossip among the passengers, but you and Captain Scorer must see that it never starts."

"Believe me, I have no wish to circulate anything so un-pleasant, anything that disturbs the holiday spirit so much."

"To hell with your holiday spirit and your cruisers and the whole bloody outfit. This is murder and I mean to bring it home. So for God's sake keep your mouth shut and tell Scorer to do the same."

"You make me think you know more than you're willing to say."

"Think what you bloody well like. Think I killed Leacock, if you like, or that Lady Spittals did . . ."

"What has Lady Spittals to do with it?"

"Nothing. I'm trying to make you see how ridiculous you can be. I don't mind what you think about Leacock or anything else, only if you talk about it, you'll never organize another cruise. I promise you that. Do you know a woman named Grahame-Willows?"

"Yes. Sits near me in the dining room."

"I thought so. She's stocked with misinformation that can only have come from you. So hold her off, for God's sake. Tell her that Leacock has been taken to hospital, run over, whatever you like, but don't let her catch a hint of what I've told you."

"Does she gossip much?"

"She lives on it and sustains half the other passengers on it too."

"She seemed a very harmless person."

"She's dangerous, I tell you. There's just a chance, Porteous, *just* a chance, that if you keep your mouth shut I shall get the murderer arrested. It's a slim chance, because there's so much talk aboard this ship. But if I don't succeed, I warn you, you'll have had it. Goodbye Summertime Cruises for good. So get that into your head."

Twelve

CAROLUS WAS NOT BLUFFING. It was true, and he knew it, that if it was noised about the ship that Leacock had been killed in Tunis, his chances of a successful conclusion to the case were nil. Hitherto the bumbling allocations of Mr Gorringer and Mrs Stick's admiring quotations from the lady at the table where we sit and all the other tittle-tattle on board were faintly amusing to him; now they were dangerous. Carolus realized that his one hope lay in that most difficult of duties, now as in wartime, security of information.

Yet for him to appear serious about it, to attempt indignantly to deny whatever wild stories might be told, was almost equally unsafe. He could not plead or threaten anyone into keeping silence. His only hope was that the facts about the events in Tunis might never reach the ship. In that case he might be able to rely on the fanciful embroideries of Mrs Grahame-Willows, or the pompous theorizing of Mr Gorringer, to account for Leacock's disappearance. It was too much to hope that Leacock's absence from his duties would be unnoticed by the passengers.

His first action on the following morning was to ask the Purser for a list of all members of the ship's company who had been ashore yesterday and also of the passengers. To explain this to the Purser and anyone else who might think it an unusual request, he asked the Captain, one of the two people of necessity in his confidence, to have it explained that Leacock was believed to have met with a street accident and been taken to hospital. It was hoped that someone had seen the incident and would give evidence about it. Even this was dangerous for, as Carolus knew, to circulate a false story to cover a true one often defeated its ends. The listener to all rumours who was actually on this ship was keenly aware of the truth. It was necessary to make that listener believe that he or she was the only one to know it. That there was such a listener, Carolus had not the slightest doubt.

Moreover, if that listener thought that Carolus himself had learned the truth, his own life could be in danger. His best course of action was to show good humour in the face of any sinister rumour-mongering, as though Leacock's failure to return to the ship was in no way remarkable, an incident, as it was to most of the passengers, to be expected on a cruise like this.

When he studied the list the Purser brought him, he had a few mild surprises. The Purser mentioned with exaggerated casualness that he himself had been ashore for a short time.

"I don't suppose that interests you," laughed Mr Ratchett.

"Oh, but it does. What time did you go?"

"I've no idea. Somewhere about seven, I should think."

"And came back?

"I was on board at half-past nine," said the Purser, growing a little sharp in his manner. "But what possible interest that could have I . . ."

"Thanks for the list, anyway," interrupted Carolus. At the head of it was Mr Hugh Gorringer, M.A.

"He insists on the M.A.," explained the Purser.

Carolus nodded. He could well believe it. Next to him was Mrs Agatha Grahame-Willows. Yes. He thought so. Then Gavin Ritchie and Rita Latour. Together at last, as Carolus had noted. Dr Yaqub Ali had been ashore in the earlier part of the day but had returned to the ship soon after lunch. Alexander Carlisle, however, had been one of the last to return before the ship sailed, while Sir Charles and Lady Spittals had come only a little earlier. Susan Berry had been ashore, as Carolus knew, but he looked in vain for the name of the Second Engineer. He wondered whether the tall girl would admit to her new friendship and decided to put his list away for a time and ask her.

Miss Berry smiled radiantly.

"Yes, Mr Deene," she said. "I did go ashore in Tunis and had a wonderful time."

Carolus could not very well ask for details and waited.

"But not with someone from this old ship. I've never seen such a stuffy lot! Call this a holiday cruise? It's been more like a funeral. I went ashore alone and met a most charming Tunisian gentleman. Quite young. He was beautifully dressed and has lots of friends in England. So I say pooh to the *Summer Queen* and everyone on board!"

"What time did you come back to the ship?"

"Oh, I don't know," said Susan dreamily. "Mohammed had a car and we went out a long way. I didn't want to come back at all, but he told me at the last minute that he needed some money to have the car repaired and put some more petrol in, so I came back here."

A non sequitur, but Carolus followed it.

"Did you meet anyone as you came aboard?"

"Only Mr and Mrs Popple. They're so dull like everyone else in this ship. They scarcely took any notice of Mohammed. As for that Dr Runwell, he was positively rude!"

"How? Why?"

"He came up behind Mohammed and me just as we reached the gangway and said something to Mohammed in

some other language. I don't know what it was, but Mohammed did not seem to like it and went off without saying good-
night again. Then Dr Runwell turned round to me and said,
'Time you were on board, young lady.' I hate being called
'young lady' like that and I told him so, but he almost pushed
me up the gangplank. Not very nice, was it?"

"It may have been meant kindly," Carolus said. "You didn't
see anyone else?"

"No," said Susan. "I wasn't really noticing."

"I don't expect you were," said Carolus with a friendly
smile and went to find Mrs Stick whose news, he felt, would
be worth hearing.

It was.

"You've heard about that sailor who tried to get Stick to
go with him to one of those places, haven't you?" she began at
once.

Carolus couldn't resist this.

"What places?" he asked.

"I don't want to talk about it, only it shows what happens
to anyone who doesn't mind his Ps and Qs."

"What?"

"He was arrested by the police last night, that's what, and
locked up for goodness knows how long. That's why he's not
on duty this morning. I said to Stick, 'It's a good thing you
didn't have anything to do with him,' I said, 'else you'd be in
gaol along with him,' I said. Of course the lady at the table
where we sit knew better."

Carolus had noticed that She had gone back to the longer
and more formal title. Also that Mrs Stick seemed to find her
information less reliable than in the first days out of port.

"Why? What does she say?" he asked.

"She always knows better. She says this sailor was just walking along the street minding his own business when two police-

men came up and got hold of him and before he knew where he was they had put handcuffs on him and taken him away."

"Surely they must have had some reason?"

"That's what I told Her only She wouldn't have it. You know what She is. So I just let Her go on saying what She thought. She *knows,* like She always does. It doesn't matter what other people say."

"But her story is the same as yours in essentials?"

"Of course it is. It couldn't really be anything else, could it? Only some say it was altogether different. They say that the sailor was knocked down by one of these little minicabs you see flying about the place and taken to hospital with a fractured leg. You don't know what to think, do you?"

"What does Stick have to say?"

"I'm surprised at Stick. He's got hold of another story altogether from that Mr Medlow, the one who's not quite right in the head. He told Stick he'd seen that sailor with the vulgar name fighting right in the middle of the main boulevard with one of the fellows off a British ship in the harbour and get took up by three policemen for making a disturbance. Anyway, he's not here, is he? So one of them must be true. Where's this place we get to next?"

"Famagusta," said Carolus. "It's in Cyprus."

"I should think it was," said Mrs Stick. "I suppose She'll have something to say about that. She always does. Then we turn round and go home, I hope?"

"That's it."

"I can't say I shall be sorry, though Stick seems to enjoy himself. It's been quite an experience though, what with all that's happened. I think that's Mr Gorringer trying to attract your attention, sir."

It was. Mr Gorringer was peering impatiently through the window of the Sun Lounge, and Carolus went out to him.

"I felt it my duty to have a word with you," he said. "I have been in conversation with one or two of the ladies, Mrs Grahame-Willows, a charming person, Lady Spittals, and others, and I find the most extraordinary stories are circulating about one of the deckhands, the man called Leacock."

"Really?"

"The truth, of course, is known. The man was carried on board by two of his shipmates . . ."

Carolus looked up, uneasily.

"At what time?" he asked.

"About six o'clock in the evening, it seems. He was in a disgraceful state of inebriation. One lady, a Mrs Popple, actually witnessed the incident. The man was taken to his bunk and is probably even now sleeping off the effects of his drunkenness. Yet a variety of quite different stories have circulated."

"That's always the case," said Carolus. "I shouldn't worry about it."

"You don't think there's any connection then, between the deckhand and the matter you are investigating?"

"Not the slightest. Have you got a ticket for the sweepstakes on the day's run? If not, let's go and get one."

So Carolus marched Mr Gorringer away. But he continued to feel uneasy. It was possible, be supposed, that Leacock had come aboard in the early evening either with the aid of his mates or alone. If so, he had gone ashore again. But the stories about him were just a little too varied and too sensational. Carolus wondered whether they had been circulated deliberately. On the whole, he felt it wiser to show no further interest in the matter.

But that was not so easy when several of his fellow passengers seemed determined that he should hear more, Mr Medlow, for instance. He had actually seen what happened, he told Carolus.

"I was strolling up the boulevard," he said. "Very pleasant too. Trees, you know, and flower stalls. When out comes that fellow Leacock dressed in civvies . . ."

"Out from where?"

"A bar, from the look of him, followed by a *matelot* from the *Rothesay* that's in the harbour."

"And then?"

"Then the scrap started. You've never seen anything like it. Fight? More like bloody murder."

"But it wasn't?"

"It might have been. It took three cops to drag away this Leacock and two to get hold of the other man. But they got them both in the bogy waggon and away they went."

Mr Medlow waved his arm to indicate the departure.

"Well, well," said Carolus. "You did have a time ashore, Mr Medlow. You didn't see Leacock again?"

"Again? If you knew as much about these foreign ports as I do you wouldn't ask that question. We shan't see the poor fellow again for years, very likely. Once they get someone inside here they mean it."

"At what time did you see the fight?"

"About six, I should think. And *what* a fight! Never seen anything like it!"

"You didn't think of interfering?"

"Are you out of your mind?" asked Medlow.

"*I'm* not," said Carolus with insulting emphasis. "It surprises me that you were alone in seeing this combat. Didn't it attract a lot of attention?"

"You evidently don't know these countries. Two sailors having a fight? Nothing! Happens every day. They wouldn't turn round to give a second glance at it. Someone else from the ship did see it, though. He was standing quite near me when it happened. That fellow Runwell. Doctor Runwell, I suppose I should say. He saw it all right, though he swears he didn't."

"Did you ask him?"

"Just mentioned it casually that I'd seen him watching. He flatly denied it. Said he was never in the main boulevard. Bloody liar. I saw him, I tell you."

"As clearly as you saw Leacock?"

"That's it. Of course it will go into my report."

"Of course."

"Mustn't leave that out. Important piece of information."

"For MI5?" queried Carolus.

Medlow gave him an angry stare and after a few minutes walked away.

On the following morning they docked at Famagusta and Carolus decided not to go ashore. He knew the place with its British holidaymakers and the residents who talked about the good times in Cyprus in the past, by which they apparently meant the times when the Cypriots were so poor that they depended on their patronage. The shops were like those of Gibraltar but even more expensive and the "native population," as he had heard them called, were just as unmannerly as the Cypriot waiters who had somehow managed to invade London during the last war.

Apparently the Sticks were of the same mind when they returned to the ship.

"Farmer Gooster!" said Mrs Stick. "Not much farmer about that place, I can tell you. All you could buy was oranges and lemons and I've had enough of those on the ship. But what was that Mr Porteous doing, I'd like to know? Running about all over the place. You'd have been sure he would get run over the way he walked across the road. I thought he was the head of this cruise business."

"He is."

"Well, all I can say is, it didn't look much like it the way he was carrying on. Oh, well, we shall soon be home now, won't we? Stick says he won't be sorry, either. He misses the Company in the local, you see. He's used to that."

Thirteen

CAROLUS RARELY HAD TO stay in London. When he did, he put up at Freeman's, a small, private and comfortable hotel, whose sole recommendation seemed to be something out-of-date which the proprietors called good service. The rooms were not very large and had been furnished about the time when Oscar Wilde used to stay there with dubious companions, called by the staff "young gentlemen" when they were addressing Oscar, and "those horrible little renters" when speaking among themselves. The hotel, however, was clean and the men and women who worked there seemed to be "on stage" all the time, playing the parts of those who worked in London hotels in late Victorian times.

It suited Carolus, who wanted no diversion at that time and did not mean to be disturbed by phone calls or visits. It was not that he wanted to think, for he had done all the thinking necessary before his cruise had ended. He wanted to decide how he should wind up the whole affair of the *Summer Queen*.

On his second day home, he telephoned Porteous.

"Would you turn up in your books to find out from what address Mrs Darwin wrote to book her last cruise?"

"Certainly, old man," said Porteous. "Certainly," and after a time he came back with 47 The Glebe. "That's that huge

127

block of flats near the British Museum. Enormous place. You can't . . ."

"And Darwin? Did he use the same address?"

"We don't seem to have an address for Darwin," said Porteous. "I expect it's the same. After all they were married, weren't they?"

"They weren't when Darwin came on the cruise last year. See where he wrote from then, would you?"

"What's all this sudden interest in Darwin?" asked Porteous.

"I think he may be able to help me with my enquiries," replied Carolus, like a policeman answering an importunate newspaper reporter.

"Well, here it is anyway," said Porteous, "though I don't suppose they've ever heard of Darwin there now. Things and people change so quickly in London. He wrote from 341 Dover Street."

"Thanks. You've no other address for him?"

"Why should we have?"

"Then tell me the address of Miss Rita Latour."

"I hope you're not going to bother all these people with a lot of questions?" said Porteous anxiously. "We get cruisers coming back again year after year and they won't like it if they think someone's going to question them after a holiday."

"Just give me the girl's address, will you?" asked Carolus again.

"She lives in Bromley," said Porteous.

"Address?"

"17a Blackheath Terrace, or at least that's where she was a month or two ago. You never know with that sort. They shift about so much."

"What sort?"

"I don't need to tell you. Anything else you want to know?"

"Not just at the moment. I'll let you know if anything more turns up."

"You haven't given up the chase?" Porteous asked facetiously.

"It's a good thing for you I haven't," said Carolus and put down the receiver.

He went first to Darwin's previous address in Dover Street. Number 341 consisted of a tall building given to so-called Service Flats, an anachronistic term if ever there was one. He went up in a creaking lift, thinking that it could only be a matter of time before the whole building was pulled down to make way for the inevitable block of offices.

He asked at a desk in the hall for Darwin. The name seemed to surprise a white-haired man with a sharply defined obtruding paunch.

"Mr Darwin?" he said. "We haven't seen Mr Darwin for nearly a year when he left here to get married. He keeps his flat on just the same, but he never comes back to it. You'd think he'd have to fetch something from there once in a while, wouldn't you?"

"No," said Carolus. "But I have a feeling you may be seeing him soon. I'm very anxious to see him and I'd be most grateful"—Carolus emphasized this with a £5 note—"if you would let me know when he comes. Here's my telephone number."

"We don't like doing that sort of thing," said the old gentleman. "But I daresay it can be managed. I take it you don't wish me to mention to Mr Darwin, *if* he comes, that you were enquiring for him?"

"Best not," said Carolus. "He won't want to be disturbed."

"No. I see. I'll telephone you from here then, sir. That's if Mr Darwin comes."

"Good. Fine. See you," said Carolus briefly and went out into Dover Street.

Then grabbing a taxi, he drove to The Glebe, that architectural horror, the proximity of which to their nesting place had so much disturbed the readers in the British Museum. Here, having walked round the block to find the entrance for Flat Number 47, he was greeted cheerfully by a uniformed hall porter.

"Mr Darwin? Yes sir. He's in residence, but I don't know if he's at home just now. I'll telephone if you like, or you can go up and ring the bell."

"I'll go up," said Carolus.

"Very well, sir. Sad about Mrs Darwin, wasn't it? Very nice person. Always very thoughtful. Oh, thank you, sir. I'll call the lift."

"You don't know whether Mr Darwin's alone, do you?" asked Carolus.

The hall porter did not seem to like this.

"Mr Darwin is always alone," he said. "Ever since Mrs Darwin was brought home to be buried."

"I see. He hasn't a young lady with him?"

"Certainly not, sir. And if he had I shouldn't know about it. He wouldn't come in by this entrance. Not just after his wife had died," said the hall porter stiffly.

Carolus made for the lift, But outside the door of Number 47, he heard the sound of a pop record being played loudly from within. He waited till there was a pause, then knocked. "Rita," he heard Darwin's voice calling, "see who it is, my pet."

After a short pause, Rita came to the door in what used to be called a peignoir but which surely has a more businesslike and expressive name to be used with 'bra,' 'panties' and other terms in twentieth century terminology.

"Hullo," she said, blowing a puff of cigarette smoke in Carolus's face. "D'you want to see Guy? He's under the shower at the moment, but if you come in, I'll tell him you're here."

She led the way into a room littered with modern machinery, a television set, hi-fi pick-up, electric heater, typewriter, tape-recorder, radio and cocktail cabinet. Carolus looked about him.

"I shouldn't think you need to go out at all when you've got all this to play with," be said.

"We don't, much."

"Nice for you."

"Think so? I bought most of it. Guy hasn't much idea. Have a drink?"

Carolus thanked her and was enjoying a whisky and soda when Guy Darwin came in, fully dressed and smelling of after-shave lotion.

"Hullo. What do you want?" he asked with quite an amiable smile.

"Oh, just a few questions," said Carolus. "I'm sorry if I intruded."

"You could have phoned."

"So I could. May I have a look at your passport?" asked Carolus coolly.

"What's all this about?" asked Darwin.

"Murder," said Carolus. "Of course you can refuse to show me your passport if you want. I'm just a private individual."

"And a damned inquisitive one. I see no reason why I should show you my passport. But you can look at it if you like. There's nothing phony about it."

Darwin went to a bureau.

"The one in your own name," Carolus mentioned.

"Of course. What d'you mean? D'you think I've got two passports?"

"Yes," said Carolus.

"What's the matter with you? Playing detectives, or what? Look at that and then get out."

"Thank you," said Carolus after a look through the passport, but making no move to leave his chair.

"I guessed I should find Miss Latour here. What have you done with poor Mr Gavin Ritchie, Miss Latour?"

"Oh, he was nothing," said Rita.

"How expressive you are. I was surprised you had time for him at all. So much cabling to do. You must be glad to be home again."

"I am," said Rita. "Guy and I are going to be married, you know."

"Congratulations to you both," said Carolus. "Though I suppose you'll have to wait for a bit. For what they call a decent interval, won't you? I hope you'll ask me to the wedding. After all, I've watched it all happen, haven't I?"

Darwin seemed suddenly to have lost his temper.

"Get out!" he shouted to Carolus. "You snooping bastard. Get out and don't come round here again."

"No. I won't," promised Carolus. "I take it you'll be leaving here, won't you? Not your sort of flat at all. I suggest Ibiza. Or Crete."

"Who the hell cares what you suggest?" shouted Darwin. "I'm going to throw you out in a minute."

"When will you move?" Carolus asked.

Rita, giving a fair imitation of the proverbial dumb blonde, asked, "Are we moving, Guy?"

Carolus stood up in a leisurely way.

"Yes, my dear," he said to Rita. "Quite soon. Too many associations round here. But I'm sure we'll meet again somewhere. Funny if we were all together, *and* Leacock, wouldn't it be?"

"Leacock's dead," said Darwin.

"Yes. I'm afraid he is," said Carolus and, without waiting for any more remarks from either of them, asked, "How did you know?"

Darwin was ready for that one, anyway.

"Read it in the papers," he said. "Quite a story. Who killed the man? He was a rowdy and a bit of a nuisance, but I can't think how he got himself killed."

"In a brothel," said Carolus. "Fighting over a woman."

"But fighting with whom?"

"That's what I'm going to find out. Have you any suggestions?"

"I? Don't be funny. I left the ship at Gib. Or don't you remember?

"So you did," said Carolus. "These cruises are so confusing. Thank you for answering my questions."

"But you haven't put any questions!"

"Thanks all the same," said Carolus. "Be seeing you, no doubt."

Carolus returned to his hotel.

He found an afternoon tea session in full swing in the lounge. Perhaps swing was hardly the word, but teas with sandwiches and cakes were being handed round by waiters in uniform, chiefly, he supposed, for the benefit of American visitors who had heard about this incredible English custom. And no sooner had he sat down than he was approached by the very person most appropriate for it—Mrs Grahame-Willows.

"You see I've discovered your retreat," she said rather archly.

"Yes. Do join me."

Mrs Grahame-Willows consented.

"As a matter of fact, I asked Mr Porteous where I could find you."

"But he didn't know!" said Carolus in genuine amazement.

"Oh, yes he did," said "the lady at the table where we sit."

"I can't think how," said Carolus. "I told no one where I was going."

Mrs Grahame-Willows smiled.

"Not even Mr Gorringer?" she asked.

Carolus suddenly remembered that he had on other occasions mentioned to the headmaster that he sometimes stayed at Freeman's. Evidently this had been enough.

"You see, I knew you were interested in the movements of those on board," said Mrs Grahame-Willows. "And since I noticed a rather extraordinary thing when we landed, I made a note of it to tell you."

"Yes. What was that?"

"The blonde young woman whose name—or at least the name she gave—was Rita Latour, left the ship alone."

"You surprise me."

"Ah, but who do you think was waiting for her on the docks?"

Carolus managed to resist the temptation to say Chairman Mao or Dr Johnson and vacantly shook his head.

"You'll never guess," said Mrs Grahame-Willows. "It was that man Darwin. The one whose wife died before we reached Lisbon."

"Oh, yes."

"I managed to overhear just a snippet of their conversation," said Mrs Grahame-Willows. "They kissed, and the man said, 'Thank God you've come, darling'."

"Did you hear what the girl said?"

"Yes. She asked something about cables. Had he received all her cables, or something like that. He replied, 'Yes. Clever girl.' Then they walked away."

"How disappointing for you."

"Not really. I'd heard enough. Of course she was reassuring him about Gavin Ritchie, the young man who was rather friendly with her when we got to Tunis."

"Of course! And what do you suppose *he* was telling *her*? Or don't you think he sent her any cables?"

"If it was what I think it was, he was probably telling her how he had buried his poor wife," said Mrs Grahame-Willows.

"Quite likely," agreed Carolus, and, excusing himself, he left her in the surroundings that suited her so well and made for his bedroom.

Fourteen

EARLY NEXT MORNING THE telephone, a "period" instrument, rang in Carolus's room. He recognized the voice of the paunchy old man at 341 Dover Street.

"He's come," he said, "with a young lady. Turned up last night. Very little luggage—only a small handbag each with British Airways on them. I didn't phone you then because it was too late and I was going off duty. But you'll be in plenty of time to catch them if you come round now."

Carolus thanked him and would have started at once if the old gentleman had not detained him.

"We don't like doing this sort of thing," he said repeating the words of yesterday. "It seems like spying, somehow."

"It *is* spying," said Carolus, losing his patience. "But you're being paid for it."

The old gentleman was equal to him.

"Am I, sir? Thank you. I'm pleased to hear that," he retorted. "I'll expect you round as soon as you can manage it, I've just sent their breakfast up to them. The waiter says they've been packing. He says you'd be surprised at what they've got into those little handbags."

It was not far from Freeman's Hotel to Dover Street and Carolus was able to get a taxi, but when the old doorkeeper greeted him with that particular look with which doorkeepers

make their wishes known to clients, he said that Mr Darwin
had gone out.

"He told me he wouldn't be long. He just had to buy something. But the young lady is there."

Carolus did what clearly was expected of him.

"Thank you, sir. I ought to phone to the young lady to tell
her you're here. But I suppose it doesn't matter as you're a
friend of Mr Darwin's."

This was enough for Carolus and he pressed the bell of
Suite Number 18.

"Oh it's you!" said Rita, seeming delighted to see him.
"However did you find us here? Guy said no one knows about
this place."

Carolus did not answer directly but looked at the confusion on the bed where the two small handbags had evidently
been packed and some discarded clothes, too heavy perhaps
for the flight bags, still lay.

"Going abroad?" he asked Rita.

"Yes," she beamed. "To Morocco. We're leaving before
lunch from Heathrow. Exciting, isn't it?"

"Very," said Carolus. "I hope you have a good time." He
looked at her as though he felt shy. "Hadn't you better get
some more clothes on?" he suggested.

"If you want me to," said Rita coyly.

"Well, I think it would be wise," said Carolus. "Guy will
be back in a minute and I don't know what he will think. He's
not expecting me here, you see. Besides, if your flight leaves
before lunch you haven't much time."

Rita pouted and disappeared into the bathroom leaving
Carolus with the two small bags to which, deep under the
clothes with which they were filled, he made certain small
additions. He had barely time to light a cigarette and lounge

carelessly in an armchair when Darwin entered. He seemed to
be thunderstruck by the presence of Carolus.

"What the hell are you doing here?" he asked.

"Waiting for you. I wanted to ask you those few questions."

"I haven't time for that sort of nonsense now," said Darwin.

"No. I see you're going away. Another little holiday? How
lucky you businessmen are. Lisbon one day, Tunis the next . . ."

"Who said anything about Tunis?"

"I did," said Carolus. "I was just giving an example. Nice
little flat you've got here. Not leaving it for good, are you? I
shouldn't mind this."

"Certainly not. Short holiday," said Darwin. "Wouldn't
give this place up for anything."

"No. I suppose not," said Carolus, as if disappointed.

"And now, if you wouldn't mind, I still have some packing to do."

Rita entered.

"Ah, there you are, Guy," she said. "I'm quite ready now.
Shall we go, darling?"

"Yes. When Mr Deene leaves us."

"Oh, don't be so rude, darling. Mr Deene only came to
see you for a minute."

"Don't worry," said Carolus, and then mouthed a lie not
perhaps in its literal sense, but by implication one of the larg-
est of his career, "I know when I'm not wanted!" he said.

"There!" said Rita. "Now you've offended him!"

"To hell with that!" said Darwin, picking up his small
bag. "Come along!"

And indicating to Carolus that he should go first, he followed Rita out and locked the door behind him. The three
went down together in the lift after Darwin had said goodbye
to the doorkeeper.

"We'll meet again," said Carolus as he left them in Dover Street.

Five minutes later, Carolus was in a public call box. He had asked for the Chief Security Officer at Heathrow.

"I've got some information for you," he said, "and I'm speaking from a call box. So don't attempt to have the call traced or you won't get all the information."

There was a short hesitation, then—

"All right. Go ahead."

"There is going to be an attempt at hijacking the 414 flight to Tangier, leaving Heathrow at 12.42," said Carolus.

"414 at 12.42," repeated the C.S.O., seemingly writing down the details. Carolus wondered whether he was accustomed to this sort of thing.

"It will be made by a man and a woman, with passports probably in the names of Guy Darwin and Rita Latour. But they may have false passports. In any case they are both armed."

"Are you sure?"

"Of course I'm sure. Do you think this is a practical joke? Each has a small automatic at the bottom of their flight bags."

"That will be found in any case."

"I daresay. But I wanted to make certain of it."

"Where are you speaking from?"

"As if you didn't know. You've had that checked. I'm expecting your men at the door of the call-box at any minute."

"Do you wish to give your name?"

"I don't mind, provided you phone through to Deputy Chief Inspector John Moore at CID headquarters," said Carolus. "And tell your men to take me to him. I don't want to waste a lot of time. My name's Carolus Deene."

"Carolus Deene," repeated the other slowly as he wrote it down. "Does the DCI know you, sir?"

"Intimately. Ah, I see your men coming along now. They haven't hurried, have they? But you'd better get a move on to prevent those two getting on the Tangier plane."

It took Carolus a good deal of protestation before he was finally taken to John Moore's office, and it must have been nearly twelve before he was sitting there, supplied with the invariable—and at that time not particularly welcome—cup of tea.

"Television's to blame for this," said Carolus indicating his cupper. "And not only 'Z Cars' either. I've never seen so much tea consumed in my life as BBC policemen in plays have to swallow."

"Get on with your story," said Moore good-humouredly. "I suppose it is a story?"

"It is. Yes. But first find out if an arrest has been made at Heathrow. An attempt to hijack a plane for Tangier."

John Moore put the required demands in motion.

"What's this?"

"A man called Darwin," said Carolus. "And a girl called Rita Latour."

"Intending to hijack a Morocco-bound plane?"

"No, no, no. Are they arrested?"

John Moore listened.

"Yes," he said at last, "ten minutes ago. They both had automatics in their bags. How did you know that?"

"Because I put them there."

"You mean they had no intention of hijacking the plane?"

"Certainly not."

"They were perfectly innocent people, in other words?"

"I didn't say that."

"You'd better get on with your story, Carolus."

"I will. But take extra precautions with Darwin, will you, John? I don't want him to get away, even to Tangier."

"I've already done that. Now will you go ahead? I can guess what's coming. A mass of circumstantial assumptions, leading us to find out whether there's anything in them or not."

"Yes. Up to a point," agreed Carolus. "It was all guess-work at first. But what you've just heard from the airport will be pretty conclusive when it's sorted out."

"Please, Carolus! The story! How does it start?"

"With a man and woman—like most stories. Not in the Garden of Eden, but on what was meant to be the next best thing to it—a holiday cruise. Do you know anything about a man named Porteous? You will. He runs an organization called Summertime Cruises. The name of the firm is quoted from its own slogan—'Where we go it's always summer.' On one of these a year ago an attractive middle-aged woman met an at-tractive middle-aged man. I accept the definition of 'attrac-tive' from those who profess to know. I can't say how accu-rate it is. At any rate, their attractions worked. They became attracted to each other. The only trouble was that the woman had a husband and a very rich one. So the two of them de-cided to do away with him."

John Moore repeated the last words in chorus with Caro-lus. "I could match this beginning with an old tale," he quoted from *As You Like It*.

"I know," said Carolus. "There's nothing new in the world, certainly not in crime. And for this first episode I admit I haven't got the remotest vestige of proof. I can only tell you that a man named Darwin met a woman named Cynthia Travers on a cruise and that the woman's husband, Tom Travers, a wealthy book-maker, died of a heart attack shortly afterwards. The ship's doc-tor, a Pakistani who suffered from chronic seasickness, wrote a certificate and the man was buried at sea by his wife's request."

"That's circumstantial all right," said John Moore. "And I suppose they came back to England, got married and were unhappy ever after?"

"Right, but before that we come on the first novelty in this case. A Mephistopheles called Leacock. What is more, a maritime Mephistopheles, a deckhand. How far Leacock was concerned in the first murder, or believed murder, or whether he came by chance on some proof of it, we shall never know now. What we do know is that it was enough to enable him to blackmail the man Darwin, if not the woman."

"I see. A serpent in the Garden."

"And a very dangerous one. I think the plot that follows is more than half his. Darwin may have been a willing partner and his claim to have been in love with Cynthia Travers, the widow of Tom Travers whom he made his wife, was obviously exaggerated, perhaps phony altogether. At any rate, he worked out a way with Leacock to murder her without, as they thought, any great risk to themselves.

"The plan was that Darwin, having made sure that Cynthia inherited all Tom's money, thus becoming a very rich woman even after death duties were paid, should suggest a sentimental return to the *Summer Queen* for a cruise which would be more or less a repetition of the one on which they had met. Darwin would then have a business appointment which would keep him from starting the cruise with his wife, but would promise to fly out to Lisbon, the first port of call, to join her. All this worked smoothly, or would have done if a lunatic named Medlow had not started sending anonymous letters to the cruise organizer, the man Porteous, which caused him to call me in, so that I became what is known in the jargon of this form of travel a 'cruiser,' along with Mrs Darwin and the rest and met the man Leacock on the first night out.

"The plan, a simple one, was for Darwin to come aboard on the night before the ship sailed and take up his quarters in one of the lifeboats. Only after it was too late did I remember how a ship on which I travelled had unwittingly and unknowingly carried a stowaway from Barcelona to Cadiz in a lifeboat. He had lived on the ship's biscuits which are stored for emergencies in every lifeboat and he came out of his hiding place quite perkily. If I had thought of that, it might have saved Cynthia Darwin's life, but I console myself by remembering that she had certainly collaborated in the murder of her first husband.

"But the scheme went wrong, as such schemes often do, fortunately perhaps. On the first night out Darwin told Leacock that he could not stand being shut up in a lifeboat a moment longer and Leacock let him out on deck for a breather. No one was about except a Mrs Grahame-Willows who had been on the cruise a year before. Darwin was convinced he'd been seen, if not recognized, so that he and Leacock had to improvise. In actual fact, Mrs Grahame-Willows had only glimpsed him turning a corner and had not recognized him at all. Improvisation is always a tricky business, since it means a departure from the original plan, and what they cooked up was not a wise proceeding at all. They argued that the 'extra passenger' must go overboard so that a search would not be made for a stowaway. Something was thrown down: a raincoat, jacket and shoes were left on deck and Leacock shouted 'Man Overboard!' loud enough to attract the attention not only of Captain Scorer who was on the Bridge, but also of the Owner, as we may as well call Porteous. I got in on their conference, much to the annoyance of at least two of them, and realized how much Porteous's determination to keep anything from the passengers 'for fear of spoiling their enjoyment' would aid any mischief that might be going on.

"Beyond being pretty certain that the 'Man Overboard' story was a fake, I formed no conclusions at this time.

"But the next night something happened which was more melodramatic and silly. Darwin decided that he must let his wife know he was on board. What story he meant to tell her

to explain his hiding in a lifeboat, I don't know, but Leacock
found out which cabin had been allotted to her. Then Darwin
(with a beard, if you please), slipped on a jacket taken from a
peg of one of the stewards, and went down.

"'Imagine his surprise,' as the storytellers say, when he entered the cabin and found not his wife but Mrs Grahame-Willows sitting up in bed. They stared at each other and it seemed
that the lady was hypnotized into silence and Darwin was able
to escape. I imagine, however, that Leacock gave Mrs Darwin
the necessary warning that Darwin was on board, since during
the next night while the ship was in the Tagus, the woman was
not only not surprised when Darwin came to her cabin, but
opened the door for him to come in and strangle her."

"That's what you think, Carolus?"

"There's more to come. But I'm pretty certain of all that.
Cynthia Darwin's strangled body was found by an old lover
of hers called Runwell. He gave the alarm too late since Darwin had already gone ashore, but you can probably prove
that by checking with Interpol in Lisbon. On the last call of
the *Summer Queen*, Leacock had bribed a man called Costa
Neves to come out to the ship at night while she lay in the
Tagus and take Darwin off. Costa Neves was a clerk in the
agent's office so he could do this without raising too many
questions either on board or ashore, but he had two boatmen
who will probably break down under questioning."

"That would be conclusive, you think?"

"With all the rest of it, yes. Anyhow that's not my job. I
simply tell you that Darwin was out at the airport bright and
early to mix with the passengers of the plane coming from London, and so be 'met arriving' by Costa Neves sent by the ship's
Purser. After that it was all what we seamen call plain sailing."

"You seamen don't explain how Darwin took the news of
his own murder of his wife," John Moore said.

"Very convincingly. He's a clever actor. But he could not appear on the passenger list of the plane for the very simple reason that neither he, nor anyone like him, travelled on it. Another point for you to check."

"Quite. What next?"

"Next Leacock got drunk as he frequently did and was indiscreet enough to have one hell of an argument with Darwin on the night before we reached Gibraltar. Perhaps he wanted paying off in advance. I heard a little of that argument. Leacock was too drunk to give any reliable indication of its nature but I'm pretty sure he was blackmailing Darwin. And what happened later in Tunis helps to confirm it."

"What happened later in Tunis?"

"Leacock was murdered," said Carolus simply. "He went ashore in Tunis regularly every trip and patronized the same brothel. Darwin, like everyone else, was aware of this, since Leacock made no secret of it. All Darwin had to do was to fly out to Tunis and, posing as another sailor, pick a quarrel with him. By keeping sober and preparing his strokes he was sure of ridding himself of Leacock and his blackmail forever. I actually saw the body of Leacock when Darwin had finished with it. And the Tunis police are doubtless trying to identify the 'fellow seafaring man' who is supposed to have done it and perhaps blaming one of the British *matelots* who were in the town that night."

"So that, you think, winds it all up nicely?"

"Yes, John. Of course you'll have to do a bit of confirmation here and there before you charge Darwin . . ."

"That's an understatement. I suppose it's why you managed to put him in our hands now?"

"Yes. He thought he was in the clear in London. I must say I was rather afraid that he would get word from someone on board that it was I who had found Leacock's body and might suspect him, but I think I managed to avoid this. He had a girl on the cruise cabling to him all the way home, but you've no idea how rumours fly on a cruise like that and they helped me to confuse the issue. I'm sure he had no idea he was suspected till I called on him yesterday and practically told him so. I wanted him to make a bolt for it. You people take so much convincing."

"If your remote and remarkable theory has any relation with the truth, Carolus, it will be the only case I remember in which the guilty came by their own punishment. Cynthia Travers was murdered when she had collaborated, you say, in the murder of her husband, and Leacock was murdered for planning it."

"Yes. And now Darwin. Fifteen years at least, I should say, for the two murders."

"Sentences are unpredictable," said John Moore, "but I should think at least he must be cursing himself for waiting for the blonde instead of getting away!"

"Why Tangier, I wonder?" said Carolus.

"There's no extradition agreement with Morocco," John Moore told him.

"A lot that would help!" said Carolus. "You know the procedure perfectly well. There's no extradition agreement— it's much simpler than that. If the British police want a man back the Moroccans simply arrest him, tell him he's not wanted and put him on the Gibraltar ferry. When it comes to Gibraltar, which is still English, he's arrested and put on a plane for London. No need for an extradition agreement!"

"There's one weak point in your reasoning though, Carolus. If Darwin flew out to Tunis on the night before the *Summer Queen* came into port there, his name would be on the list of flight passengers and unless he had a duplicate passport under another name it will be too easy."

"He had," said Carolus, smiling. "Quite another name. He must have got it years before when he could afford to be funny. I checked with the airline this morning."

"Why? What other name?"

Carolus grinned,

"Thomas Huxley," he said and left John Moore to realize what had amused him.

1-05

FINES 10¢ PER DAY